TWIN TRUTHS

Published by The Dome Press, 2018

A CIP catalogue record for this book is available from the British Library
ISBN 978-0-9956723-9-0

The Dome Press
23 Cecil Court
London WC2N 4EZ

www.thedomepress.com

Printed and bound in Great Britain by Clays., St. Ives PLC
Typeset in Garamond by Elaine Sharples

MIX
Paper from
responsible sources
FSC® C110794

TWIN TRUTHS

SHELAN RODGER

THE
DOME
PRESS

For Bull

'Between moments an "I" walks.'
Cruden Rodger

PART ONE

CHAPTER 1

They say drowning is a good way to die, that panic quickly gives way to the best high you'll ever have, but I don't believe it.

I love swimming. It empties me. There was a time we would swim further and further out, daring each other on, until the shore looked like the sky and white foam meant the end of the reef was only yards away. We knew not to go beyond the white line. We knew that the water beyond the reef would no longer protect us and sharks watched, but sheltered by the reef we were fearless.

The day I learnt the true meaning of panic, I was in a swimming pool, not thinking, just stroking gently through the water, marking the symmetry of length upon length with blurred goggle vision. Cool, calming, muffling water. Then it happened. The breath I was holding left my body and I found myself gasping inexplicably for air.

Something seemed to be pulling me downwards. I felt myself sinking, plunging, vaguely aware that the air was above me and yet unable to control my limbs, plummeting deeper under the surface. I tried to scream. I had passed the white line. I was being sucked down into the depths of the ocean, no air, down and down into the devil's throat.

3

When I came to, I was cold and shivering. There were people around me. I was wrapped in something warm and lifted onto a stretcher. The doctors never knew what had caused the fit in the water.

* * *

But that was a lifetime ago. Today was just another day in my new life. I went through the motions of normality, stepping out of the air-conditioned skyscraper where I worked into the noisy sauna of Buenos Aires street life. I hailed one of the black and yellow taxis and sank into the back seat, thankful for the sound of tango on the radio competing with the jostle of horns outside.

'Boludo!' yelled my taxi driver suddenly at an old man who had missed the change of lights and stumbled too late onto the pedestrian crossing in front of us. For a second I caught the look of helplessness on his face before the onslaught of hooting horns and raised voices. Then he stepped back onto the pavement, reprimanded; shaken no doubt, but safe.

It was a long time since I had felt safe. And yet I tried. I spent my days teaching English to middle managers in downtown Buenos Aires. They found me quirky, I think, optimistic and just mysterious enough to be interesting. Once, a local journalist interviewed me for an article on English people living in Buenos Aires. The focus was not on the Anglo Argentine community, long since a part of the social fabric, but on a small new wave of British ex-pats and travellers. Fifteen years after the Falklands War, we were still a novelty. I was described, rather awkwardly, I thought, as 'something off a Hello Kitty sticker, able to permit herself the luxury of smoking roll-ups without losing her femininity'. My cropped black hair gave me away as a foreigner in this city of long-haired, stick-thin beauties, and yet it framed my face in a way that gifted me a certain confidence. I knew from people's reactions that my eyes were my best feature, and most of the time I relished this knowledge, but just occasionally I envied my sister the distance wearing glasses gave her.

My taxi pulled up outside the ten-storey building where I lived and I went through more motions: tipping the driver, greeting the porter in the lobby, leaving behind the shady street level of cobble stones and pavement cafés to climb into a leafless world of concrete reaching for the sky. The sound of horns and sirens was never far away, so height was at a premium – height bought you light and relative peace.

Behind closed doors at last in my rented, one-bedroom, ninth-floor flat, I slumped on the sofa with a drink in one hand and a cigarette in the other, and fought with a voice that nagged at me, like an invisible rat nibbling at my feet. It was a voice that mocked me for taking so long to do what I had come here to do and I turned to something else to block it out. I decided to answer Pablo's sixth unanswered phone message. Pablo. We spoke two languages together that helped me forget. One was Spanish, the other was sex.

'Jenny, *llamaste!*' His surprise seemed genuine, and excited me.

'Did you think I wouldn't call?' The pause before his reply said more than most of our words ever did.

'I knew you would eventually. Want to come out and play?'

I bit my tongue. Play the game, play the game. This is what you want. 'So shall I come and pick you up?' Him, impatient.

'Do you think I'm going to fall for that one?' I was firm. 'No, let's meet at the restaurant, the usual one.'

'I thought you might like to do something different?'

'No thanks,' I answered, with as little emotion as I could muster.

So I dressed in a tight black miniskirt and skimpy white top, and slipped anonymously into the Buenos Aires night.

* * *

After three hours of anticipation with Pablo, oiled by a bottle of Borgoña red wine, coffee, cognac and a great deal of eye contact, I am hungry, yet there is something about entering the place that I can never get used to. I think it's the smugness of it all, the coy yet knowing glint in the eyes of the couple who are just leaving as you step into the red light, or the matter-of-factness about the man behind the counter who asks if you want 'with video or without' and the discreet way he hands you the keys. Even in the lift it is difficult. You feel like a cliché, following in the footsteps of hundreds of others who have had the same banal thoughts as you, and you wonder who was in the room before you. Later this will be spice in your orgasm, but now it makes you queasy and you fret about whether the sheets are clean.

Click. The room is rich and red and velvet, with mirrors lining the walls and the ceiling. Now comes the interesting part, the part when your consciousness undergoes its ritual metamorphosis and, with the help of his fingers already between your legs, everything that has so recently made you want to retch, including the image on the video screen, which you switched off when you entered the room, suddenly excites you. You are anonymous, at one with the human race because you are all just pieces of flesh. The mirrors juggle images of breasts and hands and thrusting movement and before you lose the urge you come in an orgy of nameless bodies.

But afterwards, Pablo broke the rules.

'Jenny, why does it always have to be here? Can't we go to your place one day, or mine?'

The question was so uncharacteristically direct, his tone so unashamedly appealing, that a wave of tenderness threatened to drown my resolve. I tried to blink away the feeling, tried to fix in my mind the red velvet walls, remembered suddenly the old man trying to cross the street and fought back an urge to cry in Pablo's arms.

'Please, Pablo, don't ever ask me that again.'

CHAPTER 2

'Live in Brixton, with a bunch of black turd-burglars? Fuck off! I'd rather teach English!'

It was a Friday night, one of my English evenings. I'd just invested in a barbecue and some potted bamboo plants, which were lined up along the railing at the edge of my balcony in an attempt to block out the city. Being a top-storey flat, there was no roof overhead and so four of us were sitting incongruously around a table under the stars, against a backdrop of rustling bamboo and sizzling steak.

Conversation often circled, among us voluntary exiles, around why we were here and where else we'd like to be but it was just like Nick to shatter the social surface. The effect was exactly what he'd intended, and a prawn colour crept up Henry's face and gathered in a frown at his temples as he tried to decide whether Nick was being serious or not.

'Do you mind?' interjected Sally. 'Some of my best friends are . . .'

'Yuk!' spluttered Nick, his imitation gob on the verandah floor turning Henry a shade pinker. 'You patronising bitch. I bet you tell everyone some of your best friends have short legs, don't you?'

If Nick had had a hand in his own genetic make-up he would have combined his penetrating blue eyes and blond hair with the body of a long-legged god, but he was somehow just never as tall as his good looks suggested he ought to be.

Henry glared at the food on his plate. Sally looked confused. 'Your legs aren't that short,' she pleaded.

'Oh fuck off, Sally, I'm only joking.' Nick softened. 'Who's for more wine? Henry?'

Perhaps it had been a mistake to invite Henry and Nick on the same night after all.

'So where would you live if you had the choice, Nick?'

'Oh, anywhere really, as long as there's sun and good wine and beautiful girls.'

'I don't believe you're as superficial as you pretend to be, Nick.'

This, of course, was Henry. Henry the serious. Henry the caring. Henry the man who would deprive a Paraguayan maid of her sole source of income out of principle.

'To Henry, who is in the wrong place at the wrong time, doing the wrong job,' announced Nick all of a sudden, raising his glass and warming to a line of thought that had tickled him. 'To the rich minority who can afford the luxury of live-in maids, psychoanalysis, aerobics, sun beds – and English classes with Henry!'

'But he didn't know it was going to be like that before he came.' Sally, struggling, but ever faithful.

'Don't be so fucking stupid, Sally. Teaching English as a foreign language is elitist, wherever you are. How many illegitimate, under-nourished, barefoot Bolivians have you seen floating around International House in London? There is nothing charitable about EFL!'

'Well, that may be a good thing!' I regretted opening my mouth immediately. 'I mean, look at it this way,' I continued, sidestepping. 'You've got to be realistic. You're providing a tool that benefits Argentina, but of course it has to be the privileged who get that tool – one, because they can pay for it, and, two, because they have the education to be able to use it.

'Don't get me wrong,' I added, as I noticed an unsteady hint of approval in the pink on Henry's face. 'There's nothing noble about my motives for being here, I just wanted to shut Nick up!'

Nick had been in Argentina for seven years now. Twenty-five when he arrived, he had taught for two years, fallen in love with the lifestyle, the status he enjoyed as an Englishman abroad and the opportunities this gave him to avoid the more obvious trappings of growing up. Then he had left the classroom to dabble in translating and journalism.

Intelligent but deliberately provocative, he either wound people up or charmed them, depending on his mood. He loved women and good times, and his disregard for the privacy of others added spice to conversation. In fact, I admired his ability to be so probing about other people and so private about himself. Once, drunk, I had ended up in bed with him, but he had lost his erection and I had fallen asleep, and neither of us spoke about it in the morning.

Henry and Sally had only been here six months and were still coming to terms with the reality of non-ethnic, young, buzzing, middle-class Buenos Aires.

How well did any of us know each other? I thought of the journalist's description of me. It was a year now since I had come to Argentina and still no one really knew anything about me.

* * *

Too much whisky had gone, Henry and Sally had left and Nick was talking to the ceiling from the sofa.

'So what is Jenny going to be when she grows up?'

'What makes you think she hasn't grown up already?'

'Girl comes to Buenos Aires for no apparent reason, stays for no apparent reason. Devoid of all apparent reason equals not grown up.'

'Nick, you're drunk. Go home.'

'Seriously, why did you come to Argentina?'

'Do you really want to know?'

Nick had asked me the same question so many times now, and every time I fobbed him off with some exaggerated anecdote, borrowed from the latest book I was reading or the latest film I had seen. It had become a game which we played as earnestly as children role-playing doctors and nurses. He would ask questions and suggest details in sentences that started 'And I suppose . . .' or 'You must have felt . . .' and between us we would build drunken fantasies of past lives. This appealed to the side of him that refused to take life seriously, yet underlying the game was a sense of growing irritation that I was holding back the truth. The fact that he was so private about himself never really seemed to register. He was used to prising the lid off other people's lives. It came as easily to him as opening a tin can, and when he got bored of the contents he would simply take another one off the shelf.

'Yes, really, I genuinely want to know. No bullshit.'

My stubbornness had created a kind of bond between us and tonight I was tired, so I began to talk. Nick took care not to interrupt and listened with solemn interest in recognition that this time we were not playing.

I told him about the man I married, about the lack of words and the endless words, about the peace inside me, and the dreams. And then about the day he was diagnosed HIV positive and the way our words and wordlessness broke down. About the battle to make him believe I would stand by him, the slow coming to terms and the rebuilding of our lives around this knowledge we didn't want. About the way that we adapted and our confidence grew, the feeling that we were bigger than anything else, that together we would defy this thing. And then how I came home one day and found him gone. Worry, panic at first, then a phone call: dislocated, unrecognisable. My hysteria drowning in a vast, still sea; a pebble jumping on an ocean floor. Smoking, unable to eat, drawing incessant Venn diagrams inside my head in an attempt to make sense of what had happened, because if only I could understand it would be alright. But I never did.

'And so I came to Argentina – somewhere different and faraway – to get away, to forget, to start again . . .' By the time I had finished talking, the blue light of early morning was pushing down the edges of the tallest buildings, whitewashing over the concrete. Nick stubbed out yet another cigarette and rubbed his eyes.

'For the first time I understand. Are you OK?'

'Yeah, I'm fine. I need to go to sleep.'

And he gave me a big bear hug as he left the flat, as if my revelations had given him a new status in my life.

I listened to the clunk of the lift dropping to the ground floor and looked around at the aftermath of the night. Distractedly, I counted the cigarette butts in each of the three ashtrays, a habit of my sister's which had infuriated me. I collected the glasses and brought the charred remnants of barbecued meat in from the balcony. My eyes wandered, glazed, over the bare walls and I thought for an instant of a house I had once known where every corner nestled a photo, and I wished that I had grown up in that house, surrounded by warmth and stories.

Moving like a ghost in someone else's dream, I drew down the blinds in the bedroom, blocking out the now sharp, white light of Sunday morning, and crawled into heavy sleep.

None of what I had told Nick was true, but it was as close as I could get.

CHAPTER 3

Just time for a coffee before the next one arrived. 'Clara, who's next? Can you bring me a coffee?'

'*La inglesita*, Jenny Patterson. *Ya te traigo el café.*'

His eyes drifted over the photos on his desk and fell upon one of his wife, in the days before they'd had children. She was pretty, desperately pretty in the photo, and still pretty now. He knew she resented the fact that he was a psychotherapist, was jealous of the intimacy he shared with his patients. It was no use pointing out to her that the intimacy was one-sided; that he was not 'sharing' anything and that all he was really doing was prompting people to confront and deal with their own demons. She held it against him that he did so much listening to other people that he had no time for listening to her, and to a certain extent she was right. When the problems started between them he found he had no patience for them, no patience with her, yet he always congratulated himself on his professionalism.

So, it was the English girl next. It had taken time to break down both her reserve and her reservations about being in therapy. He felt that they had finally begun to make progress and yet there was still something uncomfortable about the sessions.

Ignacio was used to breaking down reserve. It operated at different levels and it took time for most patients to let go of the need to project some kind of image, be this self-made, imposed by someone else or simply what they thought the therapist would expect or want to hear. The therapist developed an ear for untruths, like a musician for an off- key note, and much of his time was spent peeling back the layers of self-deception in a patient's discourse. When this started to happen some people couldn't cope and stopped coming. Others never really wanted to be there anyway and resorted to mind games, not realising they were only fooling themselves, but most had a genuine desire to understand and did what they could to help the therapist help them.

At first Ignacio thought that the English girl was playing games, like an adolescent sent by her mother who boasts to her girlfriends later about the stories she has told. At times he had wanted to tell her to go home and stop wasting his time, but she kept coming back and, even if he never got beneath the lies, he reasoned that the sessions must be helping her.

The door opened and in she walked. Her face had a set look about it, as if preparing for the wrinkles that would slowly take root over time, but her eyes flashed with the confidence of youth. She crossed the room resolutely – almost defiantly – as if this were some form of community service she had been sentenced to. She sat noisily on the leather-cushioned armchair positioned discreetly just to one side of his direct view and, without a word from him, began the session.

'I don't want to talk about anything that happened today.'

'OK, what do you want to talk about?'

'I don't know, you suggest something.'

'Well, tell me about your Spanish.'

'Haven't we done this one before?'

'Let's do it again. You say you can escape in Spanish. When did you learn to speak it?'

'My mother was Chilean. She was only nineteen when she met my father, an Englishman who worked for the United Nations, and within six months he had whisked her off to married life in England. He loved her exotic, Latin tones when she was young and beautiful, but when she grew middle-aged and fat he grew impatient with her inability to shed her accent. He never wanted me to learn Spanish, but she would speak to me in secret, and build strange and beautiful pictures of her native land. I never learnt to speak it fluently, but it was always special. I used to keep two books, one for my dreams – my real night dreams in English – and one for my day dreams, in Spanish.'

'And when did you stop keeping those books?'

'When my father found the Spanish one.'

'Go on. What happened then?'

'He couldn't cope with the revelation that she had been speaking Spanish to me in secret. He had never made the effort to enter into her previous life, expecting her to leave it all behind. She lived in a no man's land – not English, not Chilean – and when her roots broke through the cracks he started to hate her. They got divorced.'

'So why didn't she come back after they got divorced?'

'She was too scared by then.'

'Do you see her now?'

'No.'

'Is that a conscious decision?'

'Look, can we go for a drink? I can't do this stuff in here. And that's not true about my parents, or at least it could be, but I wouldn't have a clue. I don't know who my real parents are.'

Ignacio flinched for just a split second when she asked him to go for a drink. This was not the first time she had hinted at meeting outside, but it was the first time she had been so blatant. He ignored her suggestion.

'Is any of what you've told me true?'

'My nanny was Chilean and she used to speak to us in Spanish. That bit's true.'

'Us? Who is "us"?'

'Me and my sister.'

'You have a sister?'

'Look, I need a drink. Do you want one?'

Her eyes dared him to look at her. When he did, desperate to keep his response detached, professional, discreet, her eyes held his and it was he who looked down at his notes. Still, he could feel her staring at him, challenging him, perhaps mocking him.

'Off the record?' she coaxed, mischievous now.

'I don't think that would be a good idea.'

'Oh, please!' This was not a plea. And then, with more sarcasm, 'What? In case you forget that you're a psychotherapist and we fall in love and live happily ever after? In case you find out something real about me, like the way I fuck? In case you turn out to be a real human being, too?'

'Jenny,' the name sounded strange to him, 'you must realise that it would be totally unprofessional to meet outside. It wouldn't help either of us to do the work that we are doing here. This is really just about projecting some of your feelings onto your therapist, and this is quite normal, so don't worry about it, but please try and avoid asking me again. Now, I think it's time for us to end the session for today.'

Ignacio felt inanely proud of his short speech and did not bother until much later to ask himself why.

'Fine!' The English girl's response was strangely vehement. In fact, it occurred to Ignacio that she seemed strangely un-English. 'You stay in your precious little asylum for the non-living and leave me to the street. Don't worry about me. I'll be fine. Jenny is always fine.'

And in the moment when Ignacio should have said something as a professional, or could have said something as a man, she was up and gone.

CHAPTER 4

Café con leche y media lunas de manteca. Breakfast. Sitting outside at a pavement café in fresh Saturday sunlight. Alone with coffee and papers. This was the cleanest mental moment I had savoured for a long time. Unusually, I had not partied on Friday night and I was up long before normal. I watched with interest the people who inhabit early Saturday morning in Buenos Aires.

An early-bird shopper, mid-twenties, made up to try on the latest fashion and eager to please. A blind date that night, and needed a dress that would stun, determined that being on the rebound wouldn't get in the way. I watched a dog walker approach her from the opposite direction, a muddle of dogs in tow, poodles hobnobbing with Rottweilers, all expertly held on one master leash. The shopper sidestepped to avoid them, proudly carrying his eyes on her to the other side of the street. *Yes, the right dress would do the trick!*

I browsed through the newspaper and learnt that the world continued. I wondered how to hold this feeling. The feeling was hesitant, but real, a flower just on the edge of opening up. I wondered how to hold it, but couldn't. I fought and fought to keep memory out. I tried to use a meditation trick I had once learnt, to visually close doors any time an unwanted thought tried to come in. Sorry, no visitors today. Please don't come back. Thank you. Goodbye. But the visitors came again and again . . . words of a phone call that would live on inside me forever:

Hey, how are you doing? When do you get back?

11.55 Sunday, the BA flight to Gatwick. You'll be there, won't you?

I'll be there.

OK, Tootlepips. I've got to go. There's a seriously good-looking man, quite obviously chilling out after a very messy divorce, lying by the swimming pool.

Glad to hear this trip has changed you! Off you go then, I'll see you Sunday.

Till Sunday.

Click. That was then, this was now. Then and now. So little in it really, a random transition which changes everything.

So today was Saturday. What was I going to do tonight? It was a while since I had seen Pablo, but his mood swings were becoming an irritant. One moment he was happy to be the Don Juan with the lady of the night who asked for nothing, the next he seemed to resent the fact I wasn't asking him to love me. Sometimes he would try and make me jealous, telling me about some woman he was growing interested in, thinking of having a real relationship with. So why are you still here? I would ask him calmly. That infuriated him. Yes, it looked like I was going to have to give this one up. Damn, why do people agree to a set of rules and then try to change them? Perhaps I would say yes to his suggestion of a weekend in the mountains. Decisions with a view are usually more reliable. That was my sister's excuse anyway.

That still left me with tonight, though. Nick was in love again and it was definitely a case of 'time of the month' when this happened. I couldn't face the Henry and Sally crowd. I thought of my therapist. What would he and his wife be doing tonight? Would they watch a Woody Allen film and then skirt around the problems in their own relationship over coffee and brandy? Was I too cynical? Perhaps he wasn't married. Perhaps the insight he had into other people's lives was enough.

I flicked through a mental address book and felt empty. Ana, I might try Ana. The first time we'd met was at a birthday party, milling with people, but there was something that drew me to her. She seemed to have everything and yet there was something haunted about her. You could only see it if you caught her unawares. Laughter was her drug and when she was without it she looked years older. We'd met for coffee a few times since then and a tentative friendship was growing in the pauses between the laughter. Yes, I would try Ana.

'Look, why don't you come round to us? We're having an *asado* with family and an old friend of Daniel's. Go on. It'd be great to see you!'

A barbecue *en famille,* not what I'd had in mind really, but this was the kind of thing that happened on a Saturday night if you were married with kids.

'Great. I'll see you this evening then!'

* * *

Kids in Argentina stay up till all hours. By the time the youngest had gone to bed, we were mixing wine with grass and stars. I had cantered over and around the usual first hurdles: what had I done in England, why on earth had I come to Argentina, was I planning to stay forever, why wasn't I married, what did I do here, did I have a man? In England a new acquaintance would settle for your job title to give them context.

21

Here they needed a whole life description! I told them I had met an Argentine on holiday in Egypt, fallen in love and followed him to Argentina, only to find that he was married and hadn't meant me to take him literally when he said he wished I was by his side.

'*Hijo de* –!' burst out Ana.

'Don't worry,' I added quickly, in response to the looks of concern. 'I realised fast that I had been infatuated with an arsehole, but I liked it here so much I decided to stay for a bit.'

'You English women are very strange! I would kill my wife if she was as independent as you!' Ana's husband, Daniel, must have broken a few hearts in the past.

'Well, maybe you should keep a better eye on me then!' Ana, laughing.

'And what about your family? Are they in England?' Juan, Daniel's paddle tennis partner and old school friend.

'*Basta!*' I choked. 'This is turning into an interview! I'm going to charge you for this.'

'You ignore them, Jenny. They're just not used to single women! Who's for more coffee?'

I followed Ana into the kitchen. It was a lived-in kitchen, with a cork noticeboard proclaiming the pursuits of each member of the family. There were half-read magazines and children's drawings on the table and chewed up tennis shoes by the dog basket.

'You're pensive.'

'Yes, I am, aren't I? I'm not used to seeing kids around, that's all.'

'You're running away from something, aren't you?' The haunted look was there again, but disarmingly gentle. 'Don't worry, you don't have to tell me if you don't want to.'

'What makes you so sure?' I was nonplussed by her quiet certainty. It was as if we had been friends for a long time.

'You are too brittle. It's as if you are always acting. I don't mean to offend you in any way, but that is what I feel.'

'No offence, don't worry.' I looked around desperately for a legitimate subject to latch on to. My head was spinning with the wine and the joint, and the burden of playing 'question time' was getting to me. My eyes stopped at a family photo on the noticeboard and, in desperation, I fell upon a personal question I could ask someone else.

'Why did you wait so long between having Silvina and the other two?'

Ana turned from the sink to face me and explained very gently and simply. 'Silvina is not my daughter. She was my sister's daughter. My sister and her husband disappeared when she was two years old. Silvina was found by some neighbours in the street, wearing a label with her address around her neck. We were lucky she wasn't sold for adoption. So I brought her up as my own daughter. When I met Daniel, he accepted us both.'

'Jesus Christ!' I could hardly speak. 'And your sister?'

'We never saw her again. I go to the Plaza de Mayo every Thursday with my mother and all the other mothers who have lost their children in the dirty war that nobody talks about . . . but this is just a ritual now. None of us have any hope left.'

Then she looked at me. I fought against the rising panic in my stomach. 'Hey, are you alright? Listen, don't worry, we've had a long time to learn to cope with this. Are you sure you're OK?'

No, I wasn't OK. I would never be OK. How could Ana know that the story she had offered me was quite literally something I could not stomach. She searched my face with a look of pity on hers, but I couldn't get beyond the nausea. I couldn't find the words to help me spell it out.

After I was sick, they called a taxi and Juan dropped me off on his way home.

CHAPTER 5

'Clara, who's next?'

'*La inglesita*, Jenny Patterson.'

She hadn't been for three weeks and Ignacio had wondered whether the strain of her own game-playing had been too much in the end. He had always felt that it had to go one of two ways. Either she would just stop coming one day or she would start being honest and run the risk of letting the demons surface. He hoped she wouldn't just stop coming.

Clara showed her in and brought coffee.

'So, you're back. I wondered if you had decided to stop coming.'

'Would you have minded?'

'I think it would have been a mistake. I think you were doing well. How do you feel?'

'Radiant! I've been in San Luis for a long weekend.'

True, she looked radiant. Fresh air was obviously good for her.

'So, tell me about it. What was it you enjoyed most?'

'A blow job in the hills on two different men.'

So, it was going to be one of those sessions. Ignacio was an old hand at dealing with shock tactics, but there was something

24

particularly provocative in the way that the English girl did this, not so much trying to shock him as make him look at her.

'Is that something you want to tell me about?'

'Yeah, why not? I had been having this affair with a guy called Pablo. Well, not really an affair, we just met for sex really, on and off, but he was getting impatient with me and I was thinking about putting a stop to it. But I agreed to a long weekend with him in the hills, just to make sure I was making the right decision. Anyway, when I turned up at the coach station he was with a friend. He hadn't said anything about a friend coming along and I thought, typical, this is just another ploy to try and coax me into some semblance of a normal relationship with him. I was angry with him and then angry with myself, because that seemed to be exactly the effect he was looking for. So, I ignored both of them for the duration of the journey.'

Was this just story time again, Ignacio wondered, yet she did genuinely look refreshed. He held his tongue.

'Anyway, we stayed in this run-down old hotel, in the low hills outside the town, with an old cracked swimming pool and tea tables on the lawn. There was hardly anyone there and we had adjoining rooms, me with Pablo and the friend next door. And on the first night, after a dinner during which I barely directed a word in the friend's direction, Pablo was ruthless in bed. If I hadn't been so wet he would have hurt me, and he kept whispering, "You be nice to Ricardo, you bitch." That's when I realised.'

'Realised what?' Despite himself, Ignacio was finding it difficult to control his interest.

'Because I wouldn't agree to see him on a normal basis, because he thought I was playing with him, he wanted to humiliate me, to teach me a lesson.'

'And did he?'

'Depends what you find humiliating, doesn't it? I decided to play along. The next day we went walking in the hills, with a picnic and wine. When we were on the third bottle, I said to Ricardo, "Hey your friend Pablo says I've got to be nice to you. How do you like your women to be nice to you . . .?"'

'And then what happened?'

'Hey, I think you can imagine the rest!'

Yes, he could imagine the rest. The problem was he couldn't stop himself imagining the rest . . .

'And how do you feel about it now?'

'It helped me make the decision.'

'You've decided to stop seeing him.'

'No way, I've decided to keep seeing him!'

She was laughing at him and he had no idea what she had really decided.

'So, how about dinner to celebrate?'

'Only if you agree to cut the bullshit.' The man in him had spoken before the therapist. Shit! It would take a lot to get back to the therapist now. Just once then.

'Way to go! When and where shall we meet? Oh and what should I call you? Shall I just call you Doctor?' She was laughing now.

'I am not a doctor.'

'My God, this is going to be good. You've told me something about yourself!'

And that was how he started to lose it.

CHAPTER 6

I gulped some wine to drown the taste of sperm, pulled on a T-shirt and staggered over the ridge, out of sight and earshot. It was quiet, the quiet you only get in open spaces. Gentle corn-coloured hills belied the fact that we were on the edge of the lower slopes of the Andes. Hills, grass-stumbling into plains, plains sliding into the faraway sky. The kind of spot that should make you feel at one with yourself and the world.

I felt the knot inside my chest push up into my throat and for a second I was underwater again, choking for air, but suddenly the knot broke free. I let the tears roll down my cheeks and tasted the salt, my own salt and not someone else's. It was the first time I had cried in Argentina.

When the tears had finished and I had stopped shaking, I sat watching the light on the hills, taking in the space around me. My mind was blissfully empty.

I don't know how long I sat there, but when I returned they had both left and I thought, 'Thank you, you bastards. Thank you for making me cry.'

CHAPTER 7

He sat down with his guilt and carefully put it to one side, in the same way that he usually stepped out of his own skin into his therapist's chair. He brushed a crumb off the tablecloth, as if a piece of that guilt had stayed with him and this deliberate action would remove it.

When she entered the restaurant, before she saw him, he allowed himself to look at her properly for the first time. She was not conventionally beautiful, but she was striking, and her whole demeanour was sexual. She saw him now and smiled warmly. Her face, which could look harsh, came to life when she smiled.

'Hey, Doctor, *cómo te va?*'

'Leave that out, will you, Jenny?' It still sounded strange to say her name; she had always been the English girl in his head.

'Anything you say, Doctor!'

She was like a mischievous child, and he realised how long this playfulness had been lacking in his life. His thoughts drifted to his marriage. Neither of them had been able to explain how the first baby had caused a rift between them. At first they were so focused on the baby that they didn't notice they were no longer talking to each other. By the time they had the second, Ignacio knew in his heart of hearts that this was an attempt to undo the damage that had already been done and to start again. Carolina had suffered terribly with the second and behaved erratically, sometimes hysterically. This was when she started castigating him for not listening to her and this was when he started working longer and longer hours, arguing that they needed the money. A bigger house with a swimming pool would solve all their problems. He, a psychotherapist!

'Hey, Doctor, will you join me?'

'Sorry, Jenny. What shall we have?'

They ordered a *parillada* – cuts of meat and sausage, sweetbread and crunchy intestines, which came sizzling on a grill – a large portion of chips and a mixed salad. And a bottle of Rincón Famoso.

'So, are we agreed, no bullshit?'

'I don't know what you're trying to suggest about me! Anyway, there are two good reasons for not agreeing anything of the sort.'

'Which are?'

'One, I don't think it's fair for you to use anything you have learnt about me in our "sessions" outside them, and, two, whenever people make rules, they break them. I've had enough of rules.'

'According to the rules, I shouldn't be here.'

'My point exactly and, please, if you're having marital problems or think you're gay or having doubts about your profession, I don't want to know.'

'Aren't you setting rules?'

'Not rules. I didn't say I didn't ever want to know, just not tonight.'

'OK, fair enough.'

'So, when was the last time you went to the cinema?'

She surprised him again. Somehow, he had assumed that she would carry on with the mind games; that conversation would be intense and full of revelations by either one or both of them. The fact that it wasn't, the fact that they laughed and talked about theatre and music and film, seemed to give the evening an innocence.

When he got home that night and found his wife watching a film and drinking hot chocolate, he made an effort. They chatted. They even made love.

He forgave himself.

CHAPTER 8

Two messages. One from someone at the bank, who wanted to cancel next Wednesday's class. One from Nick: did I want a drink after work? Yeah, I'll go for that, must be past full moon.

'How you doing, Jens?'

'Not so bad. Where's the lady?'

'I broke it off.'

'You surprise me!'

It was the usual Nick saga. He fell madly in love with falling in love and then discovered a real human being and couldn't cope, but tonight he seemed unusually low.

'I'm thinking of going back to England.'

I thought he was joking at first, but he was genuinely restless, felt that he was 'living a lie'.

'But you don't believe in truth!' I pleaded and felt vulnerable all of a sudden.

'No, I don't believe in "truth" but I do believe in lies.'

'Isn't that illogical?' I remembered Sally floundering at my dinner party as she struggled to support Henry in the face of all our banter and I felt a sudden shot of sympathy for her. Paradox and irony were not her thing, and I, too, ached suddenly for simple cause and effect. I forced myself to concentrate on what Nick was saying.

'No, it's not illogical at all, not if you think about it. It's impossible to know what the answer is but it is possible to know what the answer isn't. Be honest, Jenny, you shouldn't be here.'

'This is as good a place as anywhere.'

'Yeah.' Nick sounded almost morose. This wasn't like him, and I felt inexplicably angry.

'OK, so tell me then, Nick, why not here? What's the difference between "here" and "there"?'

'I don't know. It just doesn't feel like we're really *living* here. It's too easy. We're made to feel too special, just because we're English.'

'Bloody hell, you're starting to sound like Henry. Don't tell me you think it's wrong all of a sudden to have someone come in and clean your house!'

'Listen, I know you like the mind-game stuff, but I'm tired of it, that's all. I think it'd be better to live somewhere where we don't have a head start; somewhere we have to get our hands dirty to be anyone.'

'Hang on a minute.' I didn't know where this anger was coming from, but I could feel the emotion rising in my voice. 'Can you stop talking about "we"? This is your cop-out, not mine. If you feel that you can only be authentic if you're surrounded by cattle on the Northern Line, then fine, but actually I think you're deluding yourself. I think what you need is a mirror to take a good long look at yourself, and it wouldn't make any difference where that mirror happens to be. But don't drag me into it, OK? I'm doing just fine here. I like it here and I like who I am.'

Nick looked at me long and hard. 'I like who you are, but I'm not sure that you do.'

I opened my mouth, but he put a finger over it, stopping me before I had a chance to find out what I was going to say. 'OK, let's not go there, but you're going to have to accept that I'm going with a gut reaction that tells me it's time to go back.'

* * *

When I returned to my flat, I sat on my balcony with a flask of coffee and a chain of roll-ups. What exactly was eating at me? Was it the fact that Nick might leave and that I relied on his company at a deeper level than I had realised? Or that he was showing a different side to his character and in some way letting me down by betraying the character he had decided to play? If he was not the person I thought he was, then what did that say about me? What did he mean that he was not sure I liked myself? He knew nothing about the real me. He knew nothing about why I was here. Or was it simply the fact that he was going back to England that bothered me? A Pandora's box for me. I thought briefly of the man I had left behind; the man who should have made it possible for me to stay after what had happened, the man I had run away from . . .

I made two decisions that night. One was not to see Pablo again. I had toyed with the idea of keeping it going, fantasised about the sexual possibilities which San Luis had opened up, masturbated about the event that made me cry, but yes, of all the lies, Pablo was one of the most blatant.

The other decision involved Ignacio. Therapy was something you just did in Buenos Aires, like going to the gym. I had treated it like a cultural playground and it had been compulsive, like the stories Nick and I had invented about our lives for each other. But now, suddenly, something was pushing inside me, pushing away from the lies. I thought of Ana and wanted to ask her if therapy had helped her. I thought of Ignacio and wanted to ask him what he really thought about me – professionally. I decided to start taking my therapy seriously.

CHAPTER 9

'For God's sake, Carolina, pull yourself together!'

For the second time in the space of three days words escaped before Ignacio had consciously formed them, and for the second time he regretted it immediately and knew it was too late to take them back. He had always battled internally with his impatience, but he had never lashed out at her like this.

He had come home late from work to find Carolina sitting in the middle of the living-room floor, surrounded by photo albums, a box of half-eaten chocolates, a half-empty bottle of whisky and a loo roll. It was Wednesday night: the night the children were at her sister's house, the night that was supposed to be their quality time, the night that was supposed to save their marriage every week. Only he had forgotten it was Wednesday.

She lurched as if she had been physically struck and fell back against the sofa. Ignacio looked at her, trying to gauge the gravity of her response, waiting for the tears and the screaming, and searching desperately inside himself for a way out.

'I'm sorry, Carolina. I didn't mean that the way it sounded. I've been under a lot of pressure lately. I'm sorry. I forgot that it was our night out.'

He moved towards her, disconcerted by her silence, but her eyes stopped him in his tracks. The pleading look, the tear waiting to fall, the hurt he was so used to seeing in them had gone. Her eyes were dry and the pupils were hard and small, pointing at him like a gun.

'Carolina?' He tottered like a child, confused because the rules had suddenly changed. 'Carolina?'

'I don't care about the pressure you've been under. I don't care if you forgot it was Wednesday or if you deliberately did this to hurt me. The fact is that you have hurt me, you keep hurting me and I've had enough.'

'Look, we'll go away for a weekend, leave the kids with your sister and go away for a weekend, just the two of us.'

'No, Ignacio, you're not listening to me again. I said I've had enough. I want out.'

'Carolina, you've had too much to drink. You don't know what you're saying. Let's talk about this in the morning.'

'There is nothing left to talk about. Don't you understand?'

Where were the screams? The tears? The paranoia that she was the victim in their marriage? The pressure on him to make everything right? Ignacio looked at her and saw a woman he didn't recognise. She looked intensely sober; her hands were not shaking, her eyes were in control. It slowly dawned on him that she meant what she was saying.

'But what about –'

'All the time we have spent together? The children? The house?' She gestured sourly at the photo albums spread across the floor. 'Ignacio, they are already a memory for you. When is the last time you really talked to the children, or spent time at home or with me? You keep the photo albums.'

'But we made love only the other night. I am trying, Carolina.'

'You made love to someone else the other night.'

'Carolina, this is your paranoia again. I have never been unfaithful to you. What the hell are you talking about?'

'My God, you underestimate me! When are you going to learn that you don't have to take a degree in psychology to know when your husband is with you or not with you in bed? I have no idea where you were when we made love, but you were not with me.'

'And you're going to break up a marriage on the strength of some pathetic wave of female intuition?'

'No, I am going to give a name to what is happening anyway. And I am going to get out while I still can.'

He couldn't look at her. He sat in an armchair and stared at the floor with his head in his hands. His eyes focused on the Indian rug between his feet, a pattern of rust and crimson with off-white curls along the border. The lines began to blur as tears threatened to drown the image. It wasn't meant to happen like this. He looked up, feeling that she must respond to the hurt in his eyes, a mirror image of the way she had looked at him for so many months now.

But she had already left the room.

CHAPTER 10

Ana looked across the pool at her youngest daughter and commented on the fact that she would need to start watching her weight.

'Ana, she's two years old, for God's sake!'

Of all the things that irked me about life in this city, one thing I never got used to was the total obsession with physical beauty.

'So? Look at her tummy. Now is when we can do something about it!' Ana was laughing but serious.

'Do you miss your sister very much, Ana?'

Ana looked at me slightly askance. 'Yes, I miss her. Here, do you want to see a picture of her?' She reached into her bag and showed me a snapshot inside her wallet.

'My God, she looks just like Silvina!'

'Yes, that is both hard and comforting at the same time. Silvina is only five years younger now than her mother was when she disappeared.'

'She must have been very young when she had Silvina.'

'It was two weeks before her twenty-first birthday. Damn, the phone's ringing. I'm going to bring back a Coke. Do you want one or would you prefer a beer?'

'Beer for me, please.'

Two weeks before her twenty-first birthday. I thought of my own. We had argued about where to have it. In the end, of course, my sister won. We booked the basement of an Italian restaurant in London and filled it with our friends. To our relief, our mother stayed away. I tried to imagine what it would have been like to have our father there. Would he have known what to give his daughters? My sister gave me a hand-carved box and told me to put my deepest secrets in it to keep them safe, even though I had no secrets from her.

'Hippy,' I teased her.

It looked at first as though the box was empty, but under what seemed to be the lining there was a narrow velvet pouch and she had placed a photo there. I didn't find the photo until afterwards.

And then something else happened that night. I remembered the end of the evening like a beginning – the distant touch of soft hands in the night, and his manhood, waves on the shore inside me . . .

'Hey, where are you?'

Losing my virginity, I thought.

'Miles away,' I said. 'Where's the beer?'

CHAPTER 11

It was four in the morning and I looked at the ashtray in disgust. Five cigarettes. My mind was still reeling. Falling, falling, and the sound of a machine like an electric saw slicing the bodies. 'Come here little girl, I need to clean your teeth.' Shiny-faced, fat, leaning over the saw. And the bodies of women and children lurched towards him out of control. I watched, paralysed, as they fell under the blade and blood splashed over the walls and the windows. Then I saw her. She seemed to be floating, unaware of the gravity that was tugging at everyone else, unaware of the horror on their faces and the blood. And then I realised why. She was asleep. 'Wake up. Wake up for God's sake. Keep away from the saw.' I tried to cry out, but she floated past me. And then her eyes opened and recognised me, and for a split second she started to smile. Then she saw it. Her eyes filled with death and I woke up with a start, just as the blade was about to come down.

CHAPTER 12

'Where have you been, Doctor? I've been trying to make an appointment with you for two weeks.'

Ignacio fought with the urge to tell her why he had not been able to work. He fought with the knowledge that he was still in no fit state to listen to other people, and to Jenny of all people.

'I had to go away for a couple of weeks. How are you? You look well.'

'I decided to stop seeing Pablo.'

'What made you decide in the end?'

'I don't know really . . .' And she told him about the conversation she had had with a friend who was thinking of returning to England and the feeling that she needed to start cleaning up the lies in her life. Suddenly, Ignacio realised that he had been relying on her games. He had had enough truth to deal with in the last couple of weeks. He wanted the unpredictability of the sessions with Jenny, the excitement of her teasing, partial revelations. For the first time there was something dull about her. He didn't doubt that for the first time since they had met she was being honest.

'Hey, are you listening to me?'

'I'm sorry, Jenny, I don't think I can carry on with these sessions. I can't be professional with you anymore. Our relationship is too personal.'

'But we only went for a meal together, for Christ's sake!'

'I know, but a lot has happened since then. I'm sorry. I won't charge you for this.'

For a moment, the look in her eyes reminded him of Carolina. She appeared hurt, about to cry. Then something in her hardened.

'You arsehole! For the first time I come in here wanting to be honest, wanting to talk, to really talk, and you fucking lose it.'

Without even thinking about what he was doing, he walked over to her, lifted her face in his hands and looked into her eyes.

'I know, and I'm sorry. We can do something like this outside, but we can't do it here anymore. Do you want to meet me this evening?'

She hesitated. 'OK.'

CHAPTER 13

I walked out, livid. Fuck him! I wanted to run, I wanted somewhere to go, somewhere that meant something. Half-running, half-pacing, I reached the Plaza de Mayo and sat on a bench in the square which looked up at the tired face of the Casa Rosada, the president's pink house, where Madonna had played one of Argentina's most treasured symbols, Eva Perón. What other president's balcony had been witness to such turmoil? Military coups, riots, demonstrations, celebrations of war and elections and World Cup finals. The square needed crowds to breathe and the crowd was deeply engrained in the Argentine psyche. It was Thursday and the mothers were here, walking in circles with their white handkerchiefs around their heads, like some forgotten sect from the sixties. I couldn't tell if Ana was among them. People hurried past, laughing and seeming oblivious. I suddenly felt out of my depth. This was other people's meaning, not mine.

Maybe Nick was right. Maybe I should go back, but back to what? Back to who? Time was supposed to be the cure-all. Tell that to my dreams! And now this arsehole of a therapist had gone all soppy on me. What was he playing at? Why had I agreed to meet him? Fuck him!

CHAPTER 14

Jenny was already there when he arrived. She had insisted that they meet at the same restaurant as the first time, which he found strange. It was as if her life was so devoid of meaning that she needed to create tiny rituals around it. He tried to block out the last few days, the last few years of his life. Carolina had been right, of course, about the night they made love. It was Jenny he had been thinking about, it was the English girl he came in. Well, now here she was.

He wanted her to smile, but she looked straight at him as he sat down and blew smoke in his face.

'OK, Doctor, these are the rules for tonight. You can fuck me if you want to, but that's where it stops, and whatever has happened to you – I don't want to know.'

'Wouldn't it do you some good to listen to someone else for a change?' Ignacio felt like a ventriloquist's puppet.

'How could you possibly think I would want to know what your problems are? I came to your surgery about me, not about you.'

He held her gaze through the smoke. 'Yes, and it was you that wanted to bring this outside, you that tried to persuade me to meet you outside, you that needed something different. Well, like it or not, that's what you've got, so shall we order?'

They ordered. They ate. They fought like lovers, used each other like punchbags, taking out their frustrations on each other, bruising the anger and resentment out of themselves. She surprised him, again, with the ferocity of her accusations, as if he had plotted, lured her into a trap, waited in ambush until she was ready to embrace her therapy, until she needed him, and then pulled a rug from beneath her feet. Blinded by the disintegration of his personal life, forgetting the ethics of his profession, he smarted at the unfairness. It was she who had lured him outside the safety of the therapist's walls. It was not his fault if she had intruded into his dreams, into his private life. He had tried to keep her out, but she had kept on and on.

At a certain point the punches began to subside and the punchbag fell still between them. They looked at each other shyly, aware that their sparring had created a level of intimacy associated with couples, self-conscious suddenly that they had been so vehement in public.

She laughed then. 'That's the first time in my life I have argued like that with a man before sleeping with him!'

He looked straight at her and for the second time that day lifted her face towards him, desperate to tame her, soften her, hold her in his arms. 'We could do something about that, you know . . .'

She looked back at him and he longed to stroke away the aggression that still lay like a cat in her eyes.

'Yes, we could,' she said, 'but I don't want you dumping on me about your private life.'

For a moment he felt resentment bulge inside him, warning him, reminding him what he knew – or didn't know – about her. But then she smiled and the smile washed away the harshness in her voice and the red bulge inside him became a bulge elsewhere as he gave in to the vision of her naked underneath him.

'We can't go to my flat,' she said bluntly, cutting through his thoughts.

Ignacio trembled at the idea of going back to his own. Carolina had moved to her sister's with the kids and was to stay there until they sold the house, but the associations were too raw, still far too raw.

She sliced into his consciousness again. 'We could go to a *transitorio*. There's a good one near the cemetery at Recoleta.'

Ignacio wondered how many men she had slept with. 'How many of these hotels have you been to in Buenos Aires?' He teased her.

'I've got my favourites,' she laughed.

'OK, I'm in your hands.'

In the taxi she sat close to him with her legs slightly parted and her thigh against his. They stopped outside what looked like a hotel with its doors closed to the public, given away by the red light above the car park. In the seven years that he and Carolina had been married, Ignacio had never slept with anyone else. He wondered how Carolina would have reacted if he had suggested coming here on a Wednesday night. Many married couples used venues like this to sex up their flagging appetites for each other or to get away from the awareness of children in the next room, but Carolina lacked the naughtiness latent in so many Catholics. She would have taken offence.

Ignacio was about to ring the buzzer when Jenny pulled him aside. 'No, not yet, kiss me first,' and she tugged him with her into the comparative darkness of the overhang of the building next door. He realised that she needed to prepare herself. So he kissed her deeply, pulled her bottom against his groin, felt her breasts pushing softly into him, felt his hardness pushing at her.

In the lift his hands were already on her, already undoing her dress. They passed another couple in the corridor as they lunged towards their room. Inside, he peeled apart the open dress. Her breasts shone in the red light. Her nipples challenged him through white lace. He fell on her now, greedy, impatient, with only one thought in his head. She pulled his hand down and he felt the wetness of her. Jesus Christ. He struggled out of his jeans, pushed into her . . .

'No!' she cried out suddenly. 'No, not here, not here,' and as she tried to thrust him away from her, he came.

CHAPTER 15

Something in me wanted to surface. I was back in the swimming pool, fighting for air. His penis was pushing me underwater. I didn't want sex with him, not now, not here. Above all, not here.

'No!' I cried out suddenly. 'No, not here, not here.' I tried to push him away, to find air, and I felt the gush, like blood leaking. Too late. I rolled over and hid my face from him, ignored his confusion, punished him for it.

'Jenny, what's wrong? What happened? I'm sorry, I couldn't help it.'

'Everything is wrong.'

An onlooker would have felt sorry for him, would have thought me cruel. What would an onlooker know? Only one person could know. Only one person could understand. Too late.

'I'm going home now.'

'You can't go like that. Jenny, talk to me. What's wrong? Talk to me.'

'Welcome to my rules! I'm going home.'

CHAPTER 16

The illusion of friendship. Shared circumstance, shared problems, the impression that someone is listening, someone identifies with you? Or simply the effect of enough wine to make you expansive, a favourite tune in a room full of people. But when does it become friendship? When does loyalty take hold? When does someone become a stakeholder in your feelings and your memories? Shared history, dependence, suffering – are these the trappings of true friendship?

Someone was playing a guitar, people were singing, sitting outside on a warm night at somebody's weekend home, beyond the pampas, where, after ten hours' drive, the hills start to break the monotony at last. Henry had his arms around Sally's neck as she sat cross-legged in front of him, rosy-cheeked and safe. A woman sang softly to Brazilian chords which purred in the air. The competitive edge of early evening banter had subsided and people were drifting with the music and the knowledge of the night, which scattered stars and space around them. Even Nick was moved, had packed away his cynicism along with the other relics he would take with him after seven years. Tonight he would allow himself to be sentimental, touched by the gesture of a farewell weekend away with the friends who cared to say goodbye.

Had I left friends behind? There were distant school friends. A girl who had Donny Osmond posters on her bedroom wall. The gorgeous brother of another girlfriend who showed me his willy at the age of eight and then confided in me years later about his impotence. University friends, reunions cemented by old laughter and the same anecdotes played like a favourite tune over and over again. Flatmates and work colleagues, though only one whose words were unguarded.

And Johnny, friend and lover, the man it hurt me to remember.

But when it came to the point, friendship didn't stand the test. Didn't stand my test. Would I miss Nick? Yes. Did that make him a friend? Would I see him again if I ever went back? Probably not. Did that mean he wasn't a friend?

The human glow around us was seductive; like cotton wool clouds viewed from a plane. Part of me longed to jump, to believe, like Henry and Sally seemed to, that the cotton wool would hold, but my thoughts sank through the cotton wool and into the journey below. What would you feel? Which friends would you remember then? Would time become slow and languorous, teasing you with the last soft sensations you would ever have, air goose-bumping against your skin, your stomach circus-riding? Or would it screech inside your head, fighting the knowledge of what was happening and the vicious curiosity about how it would feel when the earth claimed your bones? I knew, with a certainty that lived inside me like a clenched fist, that it would do both.

* * *

'Hey, Jenny, smile! I'll give you my address, don't worry!'

'So, Nick, what are *you* going to do now that you're about to grow up?'

'That's exactly what I hope to find out! Let's drink to middle age, to new beginnings!'

The theatre in him could never resist a toast. His life was punctuated by raised glasses, a gesture I was jealous of and would miss, but how much did I really know about Nick? I had lied to him about myself and led him to believe he was my only confidante, but he had not even needed to lie. He managed to be so direct and intimate that everyone assumed he was as frank about himself as they had been about themselves in his company. But what did frankness tell you anyway? I felt a wave of tenderness, which was safe, because he was leaving.

'Nick, you take care of yourself back there.'

'Hey, Jenny, of course I will. You can judge for yourself when you come back.' He seemed to sense that we would probably never see each other again. 'I'll miss you too, you know.'

'Fuck off!' I elbowed him, pricking through the charm bubble he knew would wind me up.

'I will,' he said, ducking my fists. 'I'll miss your stories.'

* * *

After Nick left I felt empty and listless. It was a pleasant sensation, a new emptiness, something to focus on, and I carried it proudly inside myself. For a while I went out of my way to see more of Henry and Sally and the other English people I knew. Sally even asked me once if there had been something between Nick and me, and I basked in the temptation to say 'yes'; to break down in tears and tell her that it was only now he was gone that I realised I had been in love with him, yet it was pointless to run after him as he would never feel the same about me. Sally would have listened softly, stroked me like a cat and plotted ways of bringing us together. She would have enlisted Henry, whose job it would be to find out – discreetly by letter – what Nick really thought of me.

Even now I was tempted. Surely Nick would realise this was a game? He would write to Henry about his listless relationships in England and ask casually how everyone was in Argentina, dropping my name sometimes more than once in the same letter. Henry and Sally would read everything into this and then one day there would be a letter which would merit a meal out to talk tactics, a letter in which Nick would pour out the revelation he had had one very drunken evening that the reason his relationships were doomed was me. Sally would invite me out without Henry. She would be flushed, enjoying the matchmaker's right to be nervous, skirting round me at first, asking throwaway questions about how I felt these days, dropping Nick's name into the conversation as if it were salt on her food.

But I resisted, not because I thought it would be unfair on Sally and Henry, but because there was a chance, just a chance, that Nick would not realise I was playing.

CHAPTER 17

The night she walked out of the *transitorio*, Ignacio had felt an almost Catholic sense of punishment. His loneliness was acute and he punished himself further by imagining that this was what Carolina had felt for years. He longed to reach back into the past, to the days when she would throw her head back, laughing at his revelations about his tortured childhood, his senile grandmother who hid in bathrooms and the paranoid dog who couldn't bear people hiding in bathrooms. She had laughed at serious revelations, too, and he had felt that she would always make light of their problems. When she stopped laughing and he stopped listening, he punished her for taking things seriously and now this English girl had punished him for taking her seriously.

He thought about the role of punishment in people's lives, the way that some of his patients punished themselves with feelings of inadequacy or addictions, or imagined that they were somehow powerless victims of a grand scheme that considered them important enough to make them a scapegoat. It was the power of this sense of punishment and the guilt that underlay it which had both estranged him from his Catholic upbringing and attracted him to psychoanalysis. For weeks he thought incessantly about his life and about the part Carolina had played. He mixed images of her from past and present in a kaleidoscope of shifting emotions, fighting to order them and failing. He realised, guiltily, how little he thought about their son and daughter, and wondered what would become of their relationship now.

Guilt hung on him like beads of sweat and he laughed hollowly at the grip of childhood. At night he had wet, guilty dreams about Jenny.

He worked, holding together his own sanity at the expense of others. He talked to his wife through lawyers. He wondered about Jenny, smarting that she didn't contact him. He would have tried tocontact her, but for the fact that – worse than punished – he felt mocked.

Jenny's behaviour had turned him into a panting, premature-ejaculating adolescent. The last image he held of her was the look in her eyes the moment before she opened the door. She had dressed frantically and yet there was a controlled violence in her movements, something very cold about her panic, confirming the feeling he'd already had during their sessions that there was a deep imbalance in her. His pleas seemed to drift past her. Her eyes were hollow, unseeing, and then they seemed to laugh at him, and her cruelty stung him. This gave him an anger that protected him.

CHAPTER 18

I didn't trust myself to see Ignacio again. It had been momentary, but shocking, the feeling that I wanted him, wanted him not just sexually, but in a deeper, forbidden part of myself. The realisation that he had somehow penetrated my defences, if unknowingly, left me reeling. I tried to stop him, to save the moment for a time and a place when it would be more than just another story, but the bastard came. I knew I was being unfair, but I hated him for ruining it and I hated him still more for not realising how. I understood I was retreating into fiction, but I couldn't help myself. It was a fiction that enabled me to live. It was water on the right side of the reef and I had already been on the other side.

So I avoided everything that might mean seeing him again. Therapy, of course, but also certain bars and restaurants, the tennis club I knew he played at, his favourite cinema. Beyond these details I knew nothing about his private life in any case, so it wasn't difficult.

I drifted. My classes at this time grew more and more obscure. I invented untenable plots and relationships, role-plays between inanimate objects. I made two bank managers pretend to be a pair of shoes talking to each other. One was called Adidas, the other was Sol, and in the end it became political, with Sol nationalistic and resentful about the other's growing popularity in her country. I made a table interview a chair. Not everyone appreciated this methodology. Some loved it and learnt to see English as a plaything. I swear they benefited more from my classes than their therapy. Others dropped me, one by one.

I got invitations from married bank managers and flirted just enough to keep my income going. I lost interest in sex, smoked for England and received my sixth postcard from Nick. Every time he found himself in a different city, he sent me a card, as if this was a plot to force England into my consciousness. This one was from Liverpool and said, 'Bonked a Beatle fan here! Love, Nick.' He never told me what he was doing or how he was, but then I never asked. I never wrote back and yet it was strange: Nick was the only person in England who knew where I was. I imagined him bumping into Johnny and talking about me, but would Johnny have known it was me? Probably not.

I read *The Celestine Prophecy* and fantasised about following coincidences round the world. I waited, alert, for one that might set me on my journey. Took the rickety underground trains, which in Buenos Aires are slightly smaller than life, and studied faces for a sign. Got myself followed once as a result, but decided that wasn't it. Imagined letters misdirected to my flat, but knew they were probably meant for the hairy grandmother who lived across the hall. Closed my eyes and pointed as I walked past travel agencies in an attempt to divine the country I should go to.

* * *

But I was tied by an airport vow. *11.55 Gatwick*. I had got there early, nervous after my fit in the swimming pool. They had kept me in hospital until Saturday afternoon and I had gone straight back to the flat and to bed, feeling heavy, as if I was deeply hung over, and not wanting to speak to anyone. Johnny had brought me tea in bed and tried to talk to me, but I had pushed him gently away, sleep all I could think of. Johnny roused me the next morning and I drove to the airport, still feeling heavy. The butterflies, which are normally so pleasurable when you're going to meet someone close that you haven't seen for some time, weren't right. I realised that I was not enjoying this sensation.

I had coffee within view of the arrivals exit and watched the expressions on people's faces. There is something quintessentially voyeuristic about airports; emotions normally played out in private are on display. I imagined being a writer and creating stories around characters and events based on the brief glimpse of a stiff or passionate greeting, a fraught or gentle farewell. I would spend time at departures and arrivals for my plots. As I scanned the faces, I imagined that these were the people I had come to meet, and invented roles for them in my life. There were long-lost cousins of Indian decent in the flight from Nairobi, a lover who had revealed a heroin addiction on the night of our honeymoon . . . This was the kind of game my sister and I revelled in. We would spend hours people-watching and inventing entire rose-tinted lives. It was four months since I had seen her. We had never been apart so long.

I walked over to the announcement board. Yes, the flight had landed. I found myself a seat close to the bar near the path for arriving passengers, ready to jump up the moment I saw her. She was bound to be last, her luggage would be last, she would be stopped at customs.

I must control my nerves. The butterflies in my stomach were flapping in frantic circles, colliding with each other in a vacuum, as if the inside of my body was one enormous empty, echoing tunnel. Now, I was excited.

At last the passengers on her flight were coming through, mostly Argentines spontaneously lighting up in relief after the long hours of a British Airways flight, all blonde hair and suntans. I was straining over the barrier now, as if I could see around the corner and catch sight of her before she saw me. As people turned into view I examined them with the absurd yet typical intensity of those who wait at the arrivals point. As if, should their attention waver for an instant, they might miss the person they love most in the world; as if they need to scrutinise the features on each face to make sure they haven't failed to recognise their mother or their son. I watched. I waited.

She was not on the flight.

CHAPTER 19

Sometimes, usually late at night, it was as if she was with me. I would sit on my balcony, turning the lights and the shadows of the buildings around me into nowhere. I could hear her voice.

'You're getting it all wrong. You can't do it if you take things so seriously. You've always taken things too seriously. Relax, enjoy. Don't think so much.'

'That's easy for you to say. You haven't had to deal with this.'

'Look, it's all about temperament. You panic too quickly.'

'Fine, so what am I supposed to do now?'

'Breathe – breathe slowly and open your eyes.'

'Fuck you, I hate your smugness.'

'Do you?'

* * *

One evening I opened my eyes and saw a man masturbating in a flat almost directly opposite mine. I watched, disgusted and fascinated. The lights in his bedroom were off and his erection was lit by the flickering blue glare of a television set. He pumped away with his hand, oblivious to the fact that the French windows gave him no privacy – or perhaps revelling in this. I wondered for a moment if he could see me, but reasoned that this was impossible and, besides, he was clearly engrossed by the television screen. I looked away, horrified at what, again, seemed to clinch the essence of 'city': the ability to watch, unchecked, an anonymous orgasm from the balcony of your own home.

When I looked back, unable to contain my own morbid curiosity, he was standing at the window, gesturing at someone. He was making a thumbs-up sign. Appalled, I realised he was looking at me. I turned away and forced calm into my step as I retreated into my flat.

'Is this what you had in mind?' I reproached the other voice, ever watchful, in my head.

'Oh, lighten up. People masturbate all the time. What's the big deal?' I thought of all the times I had sat unknowingly in his view.

'There you go again. What makes you think this isn't the first time he's noticed you? What's the harm in it anyway? He hasn't touched you.'

'But it's as if he has. I didn't have a choice.'

'You chose to watch him.'

'I couldn't help it. I was curious.'

'Maybe you both were!'

'Stop it. Stop making it seem as if we were colluding.'

'OK, OK. Calm down.'

I needed to get away from her voice, from the flat, from this city. I found a coffee bar.

'Your problem is you've been spending too much time alone.'

'For Christ's sake, will you just leave me in peace? Right now, I need to be alone.'

'You think you do, but you don't.'

'Yes, I do.'

'No, you don't.'

Despite myself, I longed suddenly for conversation or a man's body, anything to distract me from this interminable dialogue. Our worst arguments had always been because she thought she knew better. I resented the assumption that she understood what I was thinking, that she understood me better than I understood myself. And the worst of it all was that she was usually right.

The scrape of a chair made me look up. Someone – a man, unusually tall – was speaking to me.

'Is this seat unoccupied?'

'No, I'm afraid it's terribly busy,' I felt like saying. I looked at him carefully to make sure he bore no resemblance to the Blue Masturbating Machine.

'Yes, have a seat,' I said.

'Bravo!' said my sister.

CHAPTER 20

'You should be careful, you know.'

'Don't worry, Ana, I'm a grown woman. I can look after myself.'

'But you're a foreigner. Men here won't understand you.'

I marvelled at the image people had here of English women. 'Ana, you know I don't make a habit of picking people up in bars, but this one's OK, honestly.'

'Well then, invite him to my birthday party next Saturday.' Ouch.

'OK, I will.'

* * *

I didn't.

'So where's the new prince?' laughed Ana as she welcomed me in.

'Fighting demons,' I replied.

'His or yours?'

Ana had not directly broached the subject of why I was in Argentina again, but as our friendship had grown, she never missed an opportunity to gently tease me.

'Don't worry, there's someone else here I want you to meet.'

'Ana, I've told you before, no matchmaking!'

'Strictly platonic. He's not over his divorce yet, but very good-looking! I've told him there's a mysterious English woman with a shady past coming tonight.'

'Ana!'

I brush-kissed the cheeks on the way to the drinks table, combining English and Argentine mores, helped myself to a very large gin and tonic and promptly nearly dropped it.

'Ignacio, what the hell are you doing here?'

'Ah, I thought it had to be you when Ana told me she had an English friend.'

'You are a friend of Ana's?'

Ignacio came from another compartment in my life, a drawer that had been closed. It seemed somehow impossible that he could know Ana and Daniel, and I must have sounded absurdly incredulous. He laughed softly.

'Yes, I've known her for years. How are you?'

'Fine, I'm fine.'

I knew I had said it too quickly. I wondered how he was. He looked different. There was something unkempt, not just about his looks, but his whole demeanour, and I realised how little I knew about this man. I didn't even know if he was married, and then I twigged that this was the man Ana had wanted me to meet and she had mentioned something about a recent divorce.

'So you knew I was going to be here?' I changed the subject in my head.

'Not for sure, but I guessed it might be you. What have you been up to?'

The question was hesitant and self-conscious, and I squashed an impulse to feel sorry for him. Why wasn't he angry with me?

'Well, I haven't dumped any more men in any *transitorios*, if that's what you mean!' I was trying to make light of it, but knew it was coming out all wrong.

'Well, I'm very pleased to hear *that*.' He had retreated into his therapy voice and I felt a pang of tenderness I needed to banish.

'So, apparently you are divorced?'

'Yep, apparently I am.'

'Don't worry,' I interjected quickly, 'you don't need to tell me about it. In fact, let's talk about Ana and Daniel.'

* * *

The next time I saw Ana, I told her the prince I'd failed to bring to her party had also failed to rescue the princess.

'Nothing to do with Ignacio, I hope?'

'Ana, what are you talking about?'

'Oh, just a hunch.'

'Absolutely not.'

CHAPTER 21

He had realised, as soon as Ana described the eccentric English woman, that it was her. Had thought enough time had passed to face her. He was rebuilding his life, slowly, deliberately, like a very old man trying to remember how to play with Lego blocks.

What shocked him was how haggard she looked. He had concentrated so hard on measuring his own vulnerability that he was staggered by the aura of vulnerability which surrounded her now. He watched her that night in the company of others and felt that he was watching a bad play. He fought the pangs of protectiveness, padding gently round her in tentative conversation. She was distant, but did not avoid his company. He left early, aware that she was still a threat to the careful reconstruction of his life.

* * *

The first building blocks had been pragmatic. In an attempt to remove himself from the associations he found most stressful, he had won Carolina's agreement (via the lawyer) to sell the house and had moved into something more befitting his new bachelor status. A flat that was crisp and clean and new, with a high-rise French window view over the city skyline, beautiful at night, sobering in daylight. He worked, ate badly and learnt to spend time alone.

It struck him that a city at night became truly international. New York, Cairo, Cape Town, Buenos Aires – if you let your eyes relax into soft focus at night, you could be in any one of them. In an attempt to process his new status, he toyed with the idea of leaving Buenos Aires altogether, of really removing himself from the associations that had made him what he was, of finding a new life in London or Rio.

He feasted his eyes on women in the street and toyed with their ghosts beneath the sheets, yet he did not seek their company. Nor did he seek the company of friends. Many, in any case, were mutual friends who belonged to their marriage; friends who, he guessed, had been claimed by Carolina; who would feel uncomfortable with the apparently unrepentant lifestyle he had embraced; who would be unforgiving if they knew that he saw his children just once every two weeks – and dreaded it every time.

Carolina, true to her nature, was unrelenting in her resolve. She refused to even meet him for a coffee or speak on the phone. He resorted to conversations with her sister to reassure himself that she was alright, that the children were alright.

'Bachelordom'. He kicked this around in the confines of his flat and watched the letters rearrange themselves into 'boredom' on the windowpane. In the end he sought company for pragmatic reasons. He became aware of an aloofness at work, which was distracting him from his patients. He put this down to a lack of normal communication in his day-to-day life and so he picked up another piece of Lego: old friends. Some he had to woo after his 'absence', others were grateful that he had not looked to them for support they were too busy to give.

Daniel he had played paddle tennis with. They had tried going out for dinner once, the four of them, but conversation had been strained and Carolina had disliked Ana. Now he found himself at ease in their company. They were the only 'family' he felt able to visit without a current of unspoken rebuke.

Buenos Aires had a way of making six degrees of separation feel very evident. For all its sprawling size, social circles overlapped time and time again. So perhaps it was inevitable that he should bump into Jenny again one day. He was grateful, at least, that he had been forewarned.

CHAPTER 22

The Blue Masturbating Machine made its next appearance during dinner one evening, catching Sally unawares.

'Good God!' she blushed. 'There's a man in that flat, masturbating!'

'For God's sake don't look at him, Sally.'

'You don't mean to say he can see us, do you?'

'I just don't want to run the risk, that's all.'

'I think you're very wise, Jenny.'

Henry, oh Henry. I wondered what Nick would have said.

'I wonder how Nick's getting on in England,' said Sally suddenly.

Funny how a man masturbating made us all think of Nick! I raised my glass in gentle reverence. 'Here's to Nick, wherever he is.' My English dinner parties were dull without him.

Over Sally's shoulder I caught a glimpse of the thumbs-up sign.

'Forget it,' said my sister over my own shoulder. 'Just ignore him. Don't let him get to you.'

'Jenny, what do you think?'

I realised vaguely that Henry was asking me a question. 'Sorry, I missed that. What were you saying, Henry? Actually, would you mind if we sat inside?'

* * *

He was getting to me. My privacy was no longer my own. I was sleeping in fits and starts. I felt as if a rat was steadily gnawing away at the boxes I'd been trying to erect around the different parts of my life. I wasn't even sure that I would recognise him in the street, yet the vision of his self-satisfied, salivating thumbs-up sign plagued my dreams. I had started to avoid my own balcony and to spend more and more time outside, in bars and cafés. I grew jumpy in supermarket queues, started to see him in innocent faces around me. My sister and I argued. She insisted that I was being melodramatic, laughed at my unvoiced fears and told me to put a cork in my imagination.

Then, one day it happened. The telephone rang and I knew it was him. I tried to beat back intuition. There was no reason why it should be him and not someone else. It was late, but then people often called me late at night. I let it ring. The answer machine was off and it kept ringing. Somewhat self-consciously, but sweating nevertheless, I dimmed the light and moved over to the balcony to peer into the blue room. Sure enough, the Blue Masturbating Machine was on the phone.

I left the flat, taking care to leave the lights as they were. By the time I had had a coffee, I had decided not to go rushing round to Ana's or to Henry and Sally's. That would be the end of privacy. I still needed my independence, so I returned – quietly, gently – and slept a type of sleep.

The next day I phoned around my friends, dropping my question bashfully into the conversation.

'By the way, you didn't happen to call me last night, did you?'

'No. Why?'

'Oh, just that the phone went when I was in the shower and I didn't get to it in time.'

A week later it happened again, only this time there was no light or television on in the blue room, so I couldn't actually see him. I shuddered to think of him masturbating in the dark on the end of a phone which was connected to the phone ringing in my room. Six degrees of separation. I baulked at the power of technology: rapists and murderers within random digital reach of every phone owner in the city. This time I cowered in my room behind drawn blinds, reaching out, uselessly, for someone who would never be there.

I missed my classes the next morning and lost another client. My income was dwindling dangerously, yet this hardly registered. The resolve that had kept me going from the moment I had decided to come to Argentina – despite everything, through everything – was shrinking. Where was my bravado taking me? Where had my fantasies brought me? To the darkness of a ninth-floor flat, sweating at the sound of a phone.

What would Ignacio have had to say about me now? What would Nick have thought? Where was the stubborn, self-sufficient English woman I had cultivated? Only an overriding sense of self-loathing stopped me from turning to anyone, talking to anyone, as if even the fear of being stalked in my own flat was preferable to the potential stigma of paranoia.

I had been punished once as a child for being paranoid. Then there was someone who understood. This time I would deal with it alone, and this time I would not risk judgement.

* * *

Then Ana dropped a bombshell.

'By the way, I hope you don't mind, but I gave Ignacio your phone number.'

'You did what?'

'Hey, don't bite! It doesn't commit you to anything, you know. He just seemed interested in making contact, that's all.'

Something bubbled up inside me, something between anger and hope already spilling into relief, and she must have seen me pale.

'When? When did you give it to him?' I knew my voice was sharp, but I was struggling with a dryness at the back of my throat.

'A few days ago. No, it must be a couple of weeks or so ago now. I'm surprised he hasn't called.'

'Can you remember when exactly?'

'Why is it so important? Look, take his number and you can ring him yourself.'

CHAPTER 23

Each time it had taken a combination of whisky and tango to create the mixture of courage and melancholy he needed to pick up the phone. Nostalgia and forlorn passion hung in the notes of Ástor Piazola and brought tears to his eyes. The whisky warmed him and armed him, but each time there had been no answer. Perhaps this was just as well. It was still too early. She was still too dangerous. These were the platitudes he fed himself over another warm, lonely, Buenos Aires night, as he tipped the last of the whisky bottle into his glass. The phone looked at him, tempting him, and then made him jump when it rang.

At first he thought it was some prank. All he could hear was breathing. Then a familiar voice coughed itself into being and the vehemence in its tones left no doubt as to who it was.

'Have you been phoning me?' Just like that, an accusation.

'Hello Jenny.'

'Forget the hellos. Just tell me.'

'Well, yes, I have phoned you a couple of times, but you weren't in.'

'When did you phone? Which nights?'

'Jenny, what's got into you?'

'For Christ's sake, just think.'

'Well, I phoned once last week. I think it was a Wednesday.' He felt a twinge as he realised it had been a Wednesday, the day that would forever be associated with his marriage and his sense of failure. 'And the previous week it must have been a Tuesday. Why, what's the problem?'

But he couldn't get a coherent answer from her, because she was laughing, laughing with an edge of hysteria, which raised the hairs on his back.

'How about a drink to celebrate?'

'To celebrate what, Jenny?'

'Whatever you like. Freedom from masturbation! Paranoia exposed! My sanity!'

'Which is where exactly?'

'Why, with me, Doctor! Shall I come over?'

'Here? Are you sure? Yes, yes, come over. Why not? I'll give you the address.'

CHAPTER 24

The first morning after was painful. Not awkward, but loaded. I expected Ignacio to have pangs about the night before. What I didn't expect was the assault my own past was lying in wait to make. When I awoke, the face I saw in those first blurred seconds was Johnny's, and then remorse flooded my system in sudden revelation of how it must all have seemed to him, how I must have hurt him. Why did he surface now? There was something sick about it, and I felt it, glue-like, in the caresses Ignacio and I gave each other in an attempt to reassure ourselves that the previous night had been meaningful.

'Who are you thinking about?' Ignacio asked me over breakfast.

I told him about Johnny. I didn't tell him that my goodbye had been a letter; that the way I had repaid his attempts to stand by me was to leave him suddenly, without warning.

'So why did you break up?'

I sought for a way to put it into words. 'He just . . . couldn't reach me.'

'And what was Argentina – a fresh start? Why Argentina?'

'Ignacio, give me time.'

* * *

He did. He gave me time. Time and patience massaged my defences. We saw each other intermittently at first and the therapist in him must have told him that the best way to reach me was not to probe, not to force. Or perhaps this was the man in him. He was gentle, too, with how much he talked to me about his own life. I was grateful, started to feel 'safe' in his company, and allowed the affection which was growing between us to swamp the memories of Johnny that still continued to emerge.

Inevitably I began to spend more and more nights at his flat, and was honest enough to admit to Ignacio that I was partly motivated by the urge to keep away from the Blue Masturbating Machine. The light-headedness which had come with the realisation that it had not been him phoning did not take away the edge I still felt on the nights I spent alone in my flat.

One evening, over whisky and the city skyline, Ignacio surprised me. 'English girl.' He pulled my chair closer to his in the twilight that safely silhouetted his face. 'I've been thinking . . .'

I felt suddenly nervous and needed to stop him going any further. 'Well, *that's* unusual. You should see a therapist!'

'Listen.' I realised how good he had become at ignoring me when it suited him. 'I don't know where this is going and I don't think you do either.'

'*This* – you mean our "relationship"?'

He ignored me again. 'But I know that we like spending time together and we are doing more and more of that, so why don't you move in?'

A moment of unfamiliar power flashed through me. Then I saw again the look of confusion and hurt on his face when I had pushed him away from the orgasm he could not control, and the power left me. 'What do you think, Jenny?' He cupped my face to make me look at him. It was a gesture that gave me comfort and strength.

'Yes. Yes, please. I would like that. Thank you.' It sounded as if I had just accepted a cup of hot chocolate.

I pondered my motivation for saying yes the next day, on a still autumn afternoon, walking along the vast brown river that cradles the belly of Buenos Aires. As I looked out across the thick water, it felt as if I had forgotten how to measure my own emotions, as if I was trying to remember a history lesson from primary school or how to make a long-forgotten favourite recipe. Was this just another lie? How much of my comfort with Ignacio was connected to the fact that our medium was Spanish, the disguise I could hide in? Should I worry more about whether he was ready for it? About what it meant for him? What did it mean for me? Did it matter that Johnny's face was watching me? Why had I said yes so readily? My sister was silent, damn her.

For all the thinking that people do, decisions make themselves. Like the decision to leave without talking to Johnny. It made itself one morning over a cup of coffee in the fog of the aftermath. I knew that he would not be able to understand, and I did not feel strong enough to try and justify myself, so I poured a garbled explanation onto paper and left.

It is easier to be direct in a foreign language and Spanish lends itself especially well to that. Having agreed to move in, I warned Ignacio of my misgivings and of the lack of control I felt I had over my own emotions.

'Does that justify whatever you do then?'

He had no idea how close that cut – or maybe he did. In any case, I moved in.

CHAPTER 25

Asleep, she looked like another person. The effort that lined her face during waking hours was gone and she seemed somehow timid, gentle in a way that could not be explained by the inevitably softening cloak of sleep alone.

It was clear that she had suffered some kind of loss, yet he wondered again and again what it was that had made her leave her country behind and come to Argentina. The brashness of their therapy sessions had receded and she seemed more honest and relaxed, yet there remained something unbalanced about her. Her mood swings were as vehement and unpredictable as ever. For all his awareness as a therapist of the lack of fixed identity in anyone's make-up, he felt that he would never even have the illusion of really knowing her or being able to predict how she would react or feel in different situations. The habit which forms people's sense of self seemed somehow absent in her. She seemed to lack an identity in the explorative way that adolescents often do, but in a way that was atypical for a person of her age. Even now, she clung to trivial rituals with a reverence which was almost distressing to watch.

In mellow moments he had tentatively suggested that she return to therapy (with someone else, of course), but she had turned on him like a street cat. In private moments he asked himself what he was doing with her. She allowed no room in this relationship for his vulnerability and yet he knew that he dared not go in too deep. He was still too raw and he knew that she would not be there forever.

One day she shocked him with a request, yet she didn't ask openly; anticipating the reservations and misgivings he would have, she ambushed him. They had been out with Ana and Daniel for a meal and, on their return, had stopped off at a bar in Corrientes. It was two in the morning, and the haze of smoke and tango muffled the voices around them.

'Do you think people need to compartmentalise to get through everyday life?'

Ignacio laughed at her conversation opener.

'Yes, I think to an extent we all need to, but the balance is what matters. If you over-compartmentalise, you start leading emotional double or triple lives and that puts you under pressure.' Jenny was looking hard at him. 'That's probably why affairs never work in the long run. You can only separate different sets of feelings for so long.'

'But there are times in your life, surely,' she interrupted, 'when it's pragmatic to build emotional walls. Sometimes you have no choice.'

Ignacio sensed that she was talking about herself, but knew better than to confront her directly. 'Sometimes it seems as though there is no choice,' he hesitated, 'but in the end the compartments will overlap. Even the tidiest person occasionally puts a sock in the wrong drawer.'

Jenny was boring into him with her eyes and he felt his muscles tense in expectation, but when she spoke it was not a revelation or confession about herself.

'Then you won't mind if I come with you on your next outing with your children?'

Ignacio's immediate response was a mixture of anger and admiration. She waited for the pause she seemed to expect and held his eyes.

'Why, Jenny?' was all he could ask finally.

'I'm not sure. I've never really been interested in your past or your personal life before.' That blatant candour again, so at odds with her inability to talk about her own past. 'But this is in the present and I know it hurts you. I think it might be easier if I went with you. It might make things a bit "lighter", a bit more natural.'

'So you want to do this for *me*?'

'Yes, in a way, but don't read anything into it.'

It was the first time that he had ever seen her make an overtly unselfish gesture and he knew he would have to agree.

The following Sunday they met at Recoleta. Carolina's sister brought the children to the park as she normally did, and barely acknowledged Jenny's presence as she rattled through Carolina's instructions for the day. In the moment's hesitation that should have been an introduction, she was gone.

'OK, kids, how about we go for a walk and then go for a Coke?' Ignacio ruffled Dani's hair, but was shaken off.

'Who's that lady?'

Jenny beat him to it. 'She's a friend of your father's and her name is Jenny. Who are you?'

'My name's Dani and I'm five.'

'And who is the other lady?'

'She's not a lady, silly, she's a girl. She's only two.'

'Does she have a name?'

'Her big name is Alicia but you can call her Ali.'

They dawdled past the jewellery stalls and stopped where clusters of people gathered to watch the street displays of tango or magic or kung fu. They laughed at a white-faced clown who mimicked people in the crowd, and Dani laughed hardest of all when the clown caught Ignacio picking his nose. They had burgers and milkshakes and Ali fell asleep on Jenny's lap.

After they had delivered them back to Carolina's sister at the prearranged time and place, Ignacio pulled Jenny towards him.

'Thank you, Jenny. Are you sure you haven't got a few children stashed away somewhere? You made it seem so easy.'

'That's Jenny for you! Come on, I need a drink.'

Three gin and tonics and a bottle of wine later, she had another request. 'This time I need you to do something for me.'

'What's that then?'

'Come to Iguazu Falls with me. No questions and I'll tell you no lies.' She wagged her finger at him. 'Just say yes or no.'

'You are impossible. Yes, then.'

CHAPTER 26

The tickets sat on the coffee table in the living room and stared at me. 'Austral,' they said boldly. 'Chicken,' they whispered. I shuddered and tucked them from view inside the travel wallet, next to the vouchers for the hotel and a flyer with its picture. Jenny, do you recognise this?

We would fly up early Wednesday morning and return on Friday. Ignacio had, of course, suggested that we use a weekend rather than taking unnecessary days off work, but I insisted it had to be like this. I arranged to be at my flat on the Tuesday night and meet him at the airport. If that irritated him he didn't show it. Was I a coward to have him come with me? Wasn't this something I needed to do on my own? Where was my sister's advice? She looked at me blankly with the shadow of a smirk, on account of Ignacio, I suppose, and said nothing.

* * *

Tuesday. Predictably, I slept badly. The hot bath, the hot toddy, failed to deceive my body and I felt my muscles rigid and alert beneath the sheets as I tried in vain to coax them into a state of relaxation. When I drifted off it was to a no-man's-land between waking and sleeping; that impossibly grey area where you somehow know you're dreaming, know what you're dreaming and yet are unable to exert any conscious control. There is a horror in that, like the moment before you pass out under an anaesthetic and can see the surgeons putting on their gloves. 'No, don't cut me up, I'm still alive!' you want to cry, forgetting with the fug of the anaesthetic that you're about to sleep, not to die. I had a no-man's-dream about diving off a cliff top into the sea and the sea turning into concrete just as I was about to hit the water. My consciousness jolted me awake seconds before the point of contact, but each time I drifted back I was pulled to the same cliff top.

With a sense of relief that daylight had come I got up, an hour earlier than I needed to, and went through the motions of a high-fibre, high-caffeine breakfast. Relief greeted me again when I saw Ignacio waiting at the check-in desk. His eyes told me that I looked terrible, and he looked down to stop himself questioning me. I could not have done this with Johnny. For all his generosity, he would not have been able to refrain from talking to me, from interfering.

When Ignacio saw me trembling as we took off, he took my hand but said nothing. As I stared through the window I felt my mind go limp. I remembered the brief, blissful emptiness I had felt on the mountainside after the tears that came after so long, prompted by the taste of unknown sperm. The emptiness now was negative: lack, absence, blank, void, vacuity. My mind reeled through a thesaurus of its own making and somehow the two-hour flight passed.

From Iguazu airport we took a tourist bus directly to the Brazilian side of the falls, where the hotel awaited us in extravagant ownership of a view to die for. Despite my heady state, despite all the pictures I had pored over, I was gob-smacked. A picture always limits. It cannot stretch from one blurred extreme of your range of vision to the other. It cannot sound and smell and engulf you. A picture, after all, is just a symbol, a metaphor for something that cannot be translated. I faced the panorama of the falls, felt the continuous rain of gentle spray and listened to the incessant crescendo of falling water, in awe of the masterly monotony of this living, breathing view.

Ignacio touched me gently on the shoulder to bring me round and I noticed for the first time that there were other people here. I beckoned to Ignacio to hold on and we watched the reactions of the new arrivals and the time it took before they snapped a photo or turned away. Inwardly I thanked Ignacio for not saying something like, 'Beautiful, isn't it?' I knew he had been here before. I knew he was not the only one who had been here before.

In a dream we entered the hotel and in a dream we wandered the length of Brazil's view of the falls.

CHAPTER 27

There was something lost and infinitely distant in the way Jenny moved silently through the day. Ignacio was at once sensitive to her need for silence and grateful, if bemused, by her need to have him there. He did not know what drama was playing in her head, yet it was clear that there was something deeply ritualistic – so typical of Jenny – in this visit. Her eyes were empty and evaded him, yet her hand sought his from time to time, and Ignacio basked in the patience and tenderness he felt towards her. Showered and cocktailed, sitting in the terraced bar of the hotel with the sunset unfolding before them, they had barely spoken all day.

'I know this is not very fair on you, but I need to do this and I appreciate you being here.' She was unusually soft, almost calm.

'Jenny, have you been here before?'

She looked at him, into him. 'No,' she enunciated, as if the word weighed in her throat. 'And yes, in a way . . . Ignacio,' she intercepted him. 'I *will* tell you. Part of the reason I asked you to come with me was because I wanted you to know, but in my own time, in my own way. OK?'

He nodded, wondering vaguely how they were to get through the evening if all conversation seemed taboo, and nervous of how she would react if he tried to make love to her that night.

They sat absorbed by the play of light and water, marinating in the warmth of evening and that uniquely modern phenomenon of utter comfort in the middle of nature. As the sky darkened, voices began to fill the spaces around them and, finally, the clink of cutlery and glasses from the dining room inside roused them to their table for dinner.

The wine seemed to relax her, and Ignacio pounced on the opportunity to fill the silence. They talked about the places they had travelled to in the past and their favourite kind of holidays. The pressure of the day lifted like a morning mist and wine oiled their conversation.

'How much do you think you can tell about a stranger just by looking at them?' she asked, taking in the room around them, now brimming with couples.

'Quite a lot, I think, but I wouldn't rely on any conclusions!'

'Let's play a game. It's a game I used to play. It's called Life on the Back of a Cigarette Packet. Do you want to play?'

'Go for it.'

'OK, you look around and pick out a couple, but don't tell me who, then you describe them, but not physically. You describe their character or their pasts or what they have been doing and I have to guess who they are. Then it's my turn.'

Once again Ignacio marvelled at her ability to surprise him. It was this playfulness he loved in her and yet, as ever, it came with a warning.

'OK,' he warmed to the game. 'Close your eyes so you can't see who I'm choosing'. He picked a couple in the far corner who seemed oblivious to the noise around them. He looked in his mid-thirties, crisp and clean-shaven. She looked younger, and wore a provocative, strapless red dress. Their hands reached for each other again and again across the table.

'Right, they're on their honeymoon. They have only known each other for a year. He works in a bank and she was one of the cashiers. It was love at first sight for her and sex at first sight for him, but he liked the ambition and confidence in her and he started to fall in love with her.' Ignacio squirmed at the trite stereotypes that came gushing out. She guessed immediately.

'Got it. The woman in the red dress and the man in khaki shorts!' She leant across the table, drawing him in, her voice a mock stage whisper. 'But what you don't know, and he doesn't know, is that she is pregnant and desperately hoping that it's him who is the father and not the one-night stand she allowed herself in a last moment of freedom two months before the wedding.'

'And why doesn't she tell him she is pregnant?' Ignacio laughed at her.

'Because she wants the wedding to be perfect. Because she's not quite sure how he will react. They've never really talked about having children.'

Inwardly Ignacio congratulated her. Professionally he knew how frequently this was indeed the case. The couple who take their vows in front of the altar, but do not touch, until it is too late, on subjects like when and if they want children or how they want to bring those children up. 'OK, your turn. I'll close my eyes.'

'This afternoon she got into his bed and they made love. When they finished he said to her, "You always give me an erection when you come near me." She thought it an odd but flattering comment. She laughed and kissed him. She has no idea that he is deciding to leave her. No idea that that was the last time they will ever make love. Well, who do you think, Doctor?'

Ignacio was almost embarrassed by the power of her imagination, though such bursts of cynicism were not new. 'I haven't got a clue!'

'Come on, you're the psychotherapist!'

'OK, let's see. I think, but I'm not sure, it's the two opposite us.'

'Bingo! How did you know?'

'Well, she seems totally absorbed by him, but he seems to be much more aware of what's going on around him. You see,' he said, diverting his eyes, 'he just caught me looking at him, but that's not much on which to base an analysis of what could just be male-female behaviour patterns! Have you thought about setting up a business in fortune-telling?'

They played on into three whiskies and Ignacio realised he was enjoying himself much more than he had thought he was going to on this mysterious trip into Jenny's past. He thought of the games she had played in their therapy sessions and marvelled at the role of make-believe in her life – potentially so positive and so lacking in the lives of so many, and yet potentially so dangerous. The line between fantasy and reality. We all need fantasy, and the lines are drawn in different places and become blurred in different ways at different times for all of us. In moments of uncertainty, Ignacio had wondered if the unblurring that sometimes happened as a result of therapy was really a good thing. Like most things, he supposed that it depended.

'Who did you invent this game with?' He suddenly felt like the psychotherapist with his patient.

'My sister.' She replied simply. He was beginning to notice that whenever she referred to her sister it was in a straightforward, matter-of-fact way that stood out from the almost extravagant manner in which she talked about so many other things. It was growing increasingly clear to him that her sister was the key to whatever trail they were following.

'Where is she now?'

'Dead.' That simple.

'Wh–'

'Shhh.' She put a finger over his mouth. 'Let's make love.'

CHAPTER 28

Impossibly, they stood on a platform at the very lip of the top of the falls, with nothing more than a rail separating them from certain death. The vacuum carved out a u-shaped gash below them. The waters of the vast river approached from all sides in gullible readiness, swept by an invisible will, undeterred by the unfamiliar thunder that filled the air. Now caressing the curved lip of the top of the falls, they slipped, eager, snake-like . . . into hell. Ignacio and Jenny stared into the bottomless crush of water, drenched in spray. *La Garganta del Diablo* – The Devil's Throat. No name could ever have been so apt.

The magic, the horror, was mesmerising and intensified by the fact that they were alone. They stood side by side, not touching, staring. At last, recoiling from the vertigo in the pit of his stomach, Ignacio raised his eyes to look at Jenny. Her face was unnaturally rigid, her hands, clenched around the railing, were white.

'Jenny.'

She didn't hear him.

'Jenny!' Ignacio raised his voice above the din. Still she stared downwards.

'Jenny, where are you?'

'There.' And suddenly she was hauling herself up, stepping onto the first rung of the railing and leaning dangerously over the edge.

'For Christ's sake, Jenny, get down!'

Something warned Ignacio not to touch her, not to move too quickly. He was sure this was another game and suddenly he hated her for using him, hated the callousness in her. He felt a strong desire to turn and walk away from her, yet he could not afford to take the risk. Forcing himself to be calm, he used his professional voice.

'Jenny, look at me. Just look at me.'

'Tempting, isn't it?' she shouted, still looking downwards.

'Is it? Does it really tempt you? Jenny, turn to me. Talk to me.'

Ignacio's body was alert, ready to grab her if her hands or legs made the slightest movement.

She looked up slowly. Then she laughed, seeing him, and he hated her for it.

'Oh, don't worry, Ignacio, I'm not going to jump, for Christ's sake!'

Swinging round, she skipped backwards and down from the railing, coming towards him with her arms open and laughing.

Ignacio felt his body relax and then tense again as he raised his hand and slapped her squarely and firmly round the face.

She flinched and turned away, striding ahead of him along the concrete walkway across the river. They waited in silence, distant as ice, for the next bus that would take them from the Argentine side of the falls back to the hotel. Like children, they clung to their own hurt and their own territory.

She broke the silence, however, on the bus.

'I'm not playing games, you know. I just don't want to talk.'

'Jenny, why did you do that? I'm sorry I hit you, I just lashed out.'

'I don't blame you.'

'So why, Jenny?'

'Look, I said I don't want to talk. It wasn't about you, it was about me, OK?'

'Isn't it always.' The words were mumbled, but she caught them and bit her lip.

CHAPTER 29

The woman in the red dress of our restaurant game must have told her fiancé she was pregnant. He was stroking her hand across the table, trying to comfort her and atone for the abruptness of his reaction, but her eyes were red from crying and a warning light flashed on and off inside her.

I looked away from the imaginary soap opera around me and into my own, searching for my sister's voice inside my head. If I had been cruel to Ignacio at the Devil's Throat, I knew that at some level I was lashing out at her. Where was the nagging knowledge of her voice and her reactions? What a place and a time to 'disappear'. It was as if her death was becoming concrete for the first time and with it the sense of purpose that was holding me together was fragmenting. What had I expected? That I would achieve some kind of beyond-death bonding, some life-giving catharsis by virtue of following in her footsteps? It all seemed suddenly desperately childish and futile, and sour tears stung the back of my eyes.

I knew I owed Ignacio an explanation. I also knew that it was over between us. The lie was shattering into tiny pieces all around me and with it my need for Ignacio. More cruelty? I had not known I had such a talent for it. The memory of how I had left him at the transitorio flashed through me. At least I had finally been able to explain what had really been going on to him. At least that had partially undone the insult, but this time . . . I wasn't sure that I would be able to explain the end of our relationship. What made me so sure it was over? This was material I could not process now; the knowledge of it simply lay underneath everything else that was happening in my head. Ignacio was part of a journey that was coming to an end. But the journey wasn't over yet.

I ordered a second gin and tonic and waited for Ignacio to join me. By the time he did I was on my third and, as he sat down opposite me, I stumbled into the long-dreaded yet unrehearsed monologue that had lain dormant in me for so long, falling upon words as if I had picked them up off the floor.

'She was the only person in the world who was always there for me. We argued, of course, but we understood each other in an unspoken way which cannot exist between two people who meet after they are born. I don't think anyone who has not had a twin brother or sister can ever understand what that means. She was part of me in the same way that my arm is part of me.

'Have you ever watched baby twins when they first take an interest in what's going on around them, when they start to react to faces and shapes and sounds? They don't react to each other, they almost seem to ignore each other, and that's because in a way they are one. You don't react to the sound of your own tummy rumbling, do you? Because she was there, I never really needed other people in the same way as others do. I never learnt to trust or invest in relationships, because I didn't need to. They were a pastime, a luxury.

'And when she died, no one was adequate. I punished those who tried hardest for not being able to reach me, for not being able to understand, for trying to understand, and no one more than Johnny. I wouldn't let him near me, I withdrew and clawed at the cage I had closed around myself, feeling a loneliness I had never known existed. Poor Johnny did everything he could, but I lashed back at him with a viciousness neither of us knew was inside me. I felt intensely claustrophobic. The cage felt concrete, and at night I drew blood from my own skin in my sleep.

'One morning, alone, I knew I would go mad if I stayed. Argentina, the place where it had happened, lodged itself in my brain as the only way out. It was a decision made by something in me that I didn't recognise. It was not a decision that I thought about or weighed in my own mind or discussed with anyone. It simply made itself. And I responded like a zombie, unquestioning. In forty-eight hours I booked a ticket, withdrew all the money I had in the bank and got on a plane to Buenos Aires. I left a garbled letter for Johnny and said goodbye to no one. I was sick again and again on the flight, and for the first few days I was utterly dazed.

'The idea, which had taken shape in the fog, was to come here, to come to Iguazu, but I needed to find some kind of calm first. I didn't trust myself. I knew I needed to achieve some kind of stability, even if it was only superficial, before I could make the trip. Ha! Look at me now! You see it's taken me more than a year to get here.'

'Have you had no contact with anyone at home?'

'Home?' I wondered briefly what it might have been like to have had a mother and father to turn to.

'No, I have had no contact with anyone at "home". I told Johnny in the letter that I would never forgive him if he tried to find me and that there was no use anyway, that it was over between us. I didn't tell him I was coming to Argentina, but he guessed and he did make one attempt. He put an ad in the *Buenos Aires Herald* and let it run for eight weeks. It said "I will not follow you, but if you want me to come, if you want to speak, just call." I didn't. I created the likeness of a life which would give me the calm and the courage to come to the place where my sister was the last time I ever spoke to her.'

The memory hung in my head, the trite exchange which had played again and again in the moments and days and months that followed the news.

Hey, how are you doing? When do you get back?

11.55 Sunday, the BA flight to Gatwick. You'll be there, won't you?

I'll be there.

OK, Tootlepips. I've got to go. There's a seriously good-looking man, quite obviously chilling out after a very messy divorce, lying by the swimming pool.

Glad to hear this trip has changed you! Off you go then, I'll see you Sunday.

– Till Sunday.

Click.

'How did she die, Jenny?'

'She was on the Austral flight from Iguazu to Buenos Aires, the one that crashed. I had a fit in a swimming pool in England and she died in a plane crash in Argentina.'

PART TWO

CHAPTER 30

Jenny was the extrovert. I was the coy one. Adjectives are dangerously powerful in the life of a twin. You are not described, you are defined – not merely 'shy', but 'the shy one'. We grew up in labels.

I didn't want to hide in the attic, but Jenny convinced me no one would think of looking for us there. And maybe no one would have done if Jenny hadn't got so hungry she decided to creep into the kitchen in search of food and run straight into Nana's apron strings. That was the way Jenny was; she never thought things through. She would have an idea, call it a plan and persuade me against my better judgement to take part.

Putting three live frogs in Mrs Grantham's desk was one of her most inspired plans and it won us lasting popularity with form 3B. Frankly, I thought Mrs Grantham deserved everything she got, but it didn't seem fair that I was always hauled in alongside Jenny as the source of the trouble. People gave us labels to separate us and treated us as inseparable in the same breath. This meant that a wooden spoon across the palm of the hand for Jenny normally meant a wooden spoon across the palm of the hand for me, too.

The day Mother caught us sniffing petrol was a bad one. We were in the garage, quietly enjoying a sniff or two from the petrol can that in those days people took in the back of the car on long journeys, when in walked Mother. The irony was she was as drunk as a skunk, but at eight years old the irony was lost on us, and what was most apparent was her anger. Swearing loudly at our father, which seemed a little unfair as we had never met him and he could hardly be held responsible for the petrol-smelling tendencies we had developed, she grabbed each of us unsteadily and dragged us into the house, where we were banished to our room without supper. A wooden spoon across the hand is one thing, but a night with no food is an altogether superior form of torture and one that caused even fiercer resentment in Jenny than it did in me.

'I hate her, Pips. I hate her.'

'But she's our mum, you can't hate a mum. Mrs Green says that children who hate their mothers are unnatural.' I was always the more conformist of the two, the more eager to please and receive approval.

'Mrs Green is unnatural. You shouldn't listen to anything she says, Pips. She has a nose the size of an elephant's willy.' Jenny could always make me laugh.

* * *

Mother told us that life had treated her very badly, but it didn't seem so bad to us. We lived in a solid three-bedroomed house with a large garden in Surrey, and we had a live-in Chilean nanny who had been with us for as long as either of us could remember. Mother worked at a lawyer's firm, and the name of the father we never knew had been dirt forever.

The trouble with Mother was that she treated herself very badly. She had these binges, where she would drink neat vodka and get hysterical, and we would cower in the TV room with Nana, who told us stories in Spanish to distract us. Once, Mother burst into the room and told us she was going to send us to boarding school, because she couldn't bear to be reminded of our father any longer. After Nana had calmed her down, she took us upstairs and told us not to worry, that Mother loved us really and didn't mean what she was saying – but she did in a way.

Then Mother met a man, and life slowly introduced us to a lesson that put frogs and petrol-sniffing firmly into the realms of childhood.

CHAPTER 31

There was something about Frank that made me feel uncomfortable. He was strong and charming and played games with us. He made Mother laugh and put his arm around her. He was kind to Nana and offered to do the dishes if he came round for dinner. The third time we met him, Jenny asked him if he was going to become our father. She thought he was wonderful. Mother even blushed, but I didn't like his eyes.

I asked Nana if some people's eyes were bad.

'No, *hija mía*,' she said gently. 'Badness is inside people and you can't always see it from the outside. You shouldn't judge people by the way they look.'

'She thinks Frank's got bad eyes, don't you, silly?'

I hadn't said anything to Jenny about Frank's eyes, but this was normal; she often knew what I was thinking. Nana used to laugh at us both and say that she despaired, it was like listening to conversations with bits missing, because we would respond aloud to each other's thoughts and it wasn't fair on a poor soul whose first language was Spanish.

'Well, maybe he *has* got bad eyes.'

'There is a witch who lives in the bottom of Frank's eyes and in the dead of night she will come and get you, woo-oo-ooh!' Jenny taunted, pouncing on me.

'Shhh, the pair of you. Your mother is happier than she's been for a long time. Let her be.' Nana was so trusting.

At first he used to take Mother out and then leave after dropping her home. Then he started to stay the night on weekends. We weren't used to having a man around the house at breakfast time, and the atmosphere was positively jolly. Frank would fry bacon and eggs in his dressing gown and Mother would gaze at him like a sick child. At night we heard strange cries coming from Mother's bedroom. Jenny told me what they were.

'Are they really *doing* it?' I asked her in horror. 'But it sounds like he's hurting her!'

'Look, I'm going to show you something.' Jenny had that glint in her eye, which meant she was up to something. We climbed into the attic, which, since the day it had served as a hiding place in our attempt to miss a day's school, had become our secret refuge and the place where we planned adventures. Jenny sat down cross-legged and ceremoniously unrolled a magazine with a picture of a naked woman sandwiched between two erections.

'I found it in the back of Frank's car,' she said proudly, in reply to my unspoken question.

When they finally got round to sex education at school we knew that as often as not women did it with two men at a time.

* * *

103

I got used to Frank's eyes. I stopped questioning them. He was fun to have around. Most of all he made Mother happy, and when Mother was happy she didn't drink neat vodka. It was the nearest we ever came to being a 'family' and at school we paraded our new-found normality, brave enough for the first time to invite people to play at our house without fear of being confronted by Mother in one of her 'moods', as Nana so gently called them.

Then Nana received news of the death of her mother and decided it was time to return to her country and look after her ailing father. We learnt the meaning of loss. Nana had provided the safety net that Mother had never been able to. It was Nana we turned to for comfort and for grown-up answers to our childhood questions. We knew, of course, that Nana had her own ties and history in Chile. We knew the names of her parents and the sad past that had exiled her and the husband who died two years after fleeing from their home country, but all this was the stuff of stories. Nothing had prepared us for the intrusion of her past into our present, for the loss, at the age of nine, of the only unconditional adult emotional presence in our lives.

My memory of her leaving is blurred. It was a time that locked my sister and me together, as we clung instinctively to each other for support. Mother seemed impervious, engrossed in Frank's attentions, either unaware or uncaring of what this meant to Jenny and me. My reaction was one of withdrawal; Jenny's was more overt. She became petulant in Mother's company, refusing to respond to instructions that had normally come from Nana, accusing Mother of sending Nana away. Frank's presence calmed us all.

CHAPTER 32

Frank bought Mother an enormous bunch of red roses one Valentine's Day. 'Yawn, yawn, there will be noises tonight,' said Jenny under her breath as Mother squealed in delight.

'Jenny, Pippa, I have something for you, too. Something for all of us.' Winking at Mother, he said, 'Now sit down and close your eyes. I am going to give you something and you have to guess what it is, but don't open your eyes until I say you can.'

I felt something like pieces of paper or a very small magazine in my hand and thought of the magazine full of naked bodies that lay enshrined beside the sheep's skull in our attic hoard of childhood treasures.

'Money!' cried Jenny.

'Now don't open your eyes. It's not money, but it did cost money. Pippa?'

'Is it a magazine?'

'No, sweetheart, it's not a magazine. It's a piece of paper to go on holiday with.'

And so went the game until the identity of the air tickets was revealed. We were all going on holiday to Cancun. In the months that led up to the summer, Jenny and I embarked on an extensive research programme, which took place as much in our imaginations as in reality. We knew that this was Nana's continent, and we plotted adventures that took us from Mexico to her doorstep in Santiago. We antagonised Mother by speaking in rusty Spanish together in front of her. We were the envy of our classmates. And we were grateful to Frank.

* * *

It was a holiday of firsts. The first time we went on a plane. The first time we went outside Europe. The first time we felt the fearlessness of snorkelling with coloured fish, of swimming side by side in endless turquoise water. The first time we heard Spanish spoken by anyone besides Nana and each other. The first time we experienced hot, wet heat and thunderstorms that blackened the sky. The first time we tasted lobster and drank papaya juice. The first time we looked like a normal, happy family on holiday.

And the first time Frank touched us.

* * *

It could have been innocent. Jenny and I had been swimming and Mother and Frank held towels up to us as we came out of the water. Jenny grabbed the first from Mother and embarked on an excited account of her fish-spotting as she dried herself down.

'Come on you, let's get you dry,' said Frank in his affectionate, rough and tumble voice, enveloping me in the towel. And he started to rub me dry. My arms, my back, my legs, my thighs. 'Rubadubdub,' he crooned as he moved his hands up my leg. I had a lightning sensation of an unfamiliar and pleasant tingling between my legs.

'There we go. I think you're done, my little Pipsqueak.'

The problem with a name like Pippa is that it lends itself to stupid nicknames. Jenny's name was much more glamorous.

I said nothing to Jenny about the funny feeling, but I wanted Frank to rub me dry again to find out if I had imagined it. I tried drying myself in the same way he had done to see if it made me tingle, but it didn't.

The towel-drying became a ritual. Frank was very fair. He would dry one of us on one occasion and the other on the next. The tingling didn't come back and Jenny never said anything to me about a tingling when Frank dried her, so I forgot about it.

Until one afternoon when Mother and Jenny had gone off to buy cold Coca-Cola. This time Frank sat me on his lap to dry me and the tingling was much stronger than before. All the time he crooned on and looked straight at me as if there was nothing unusual and nothing to be afraid of. I felt the slightest sensation of his fingers dipping under my swimsuit, a touch as swift and light as a feather, so quick I might have believed I had imagined it were it not for the funny tingling which persisted in an unknown part of me.

* * *

'Jenny, do you ever get a funny tingly feeling inside?' I asked her, finally, one afternoon. She knew immediately what I meant.

'Sometimes I get it in the shower. And . . . Pippa . . . ?'

'Yes,' I answered, without her needing to voice the question, 'when he dries me.'

'You, too, then,' she said slowly.

'What do you think it means?' I asked my big sister, relieved that it had happened to both of us.

'I think it's his way of showing he likes us.'

'I wish Nana was here. Do you think we should ask Mother what she thinks?'

'I don't think Frank would like that.'

'Do you think we're bad?'

'Not if it only happens once a week.'

And so we reasoned, trying inexpertly to deal with the paradoxical emotions and sensations such gentle abuse evoked in our children's minds, comforting and reassuring each other in the absence of an adult voice to help us understand the conflicting cycle of pleasure and guilt, fear and self-doubt that shrouds the mind of the abused child—and ensures that the abuse remains unexposed.

CHAPTER 33

Then the unspeakable happened. Even now I find it difficult to talk about it in whole sentences. I can talk around it, I can describe in words in my mind what happened before and after, I can brushstroke the scene, but the detail remains a prisoner of isolated nouns, unconnected, like a pile of tin cans on a rubbish heap.

It was a few months after our return from Cancun. Frank was practically living in our house now and the towel-drying had stopped with the end of our holiday. His presence sat comfortably between us and Mother, a new kind of safety net, which filled patches of Nana's absence, yet Jenny and I avoided talking about him, in the same way that we had sometimes observed adults avoiding each other's eyes.

Occasionally I wonder how I would have reacted if Jenny had not been there. At the time, of course, I never questioned it. At the time I clung to the knowledge that it happened to both of us. I clung to the strength in Jenny, yet it meant that there was a witness. It meant that I could not pretend to myself.

Mother told us that she was turning over a new leaf. This involved talking openly about vodka, strained shopping outings with the two of us, food that we had never tasted before, and something she called drama therapy on Thursday nights, which normally meant that she came home puffy-eyed and wanting to discuss things we found embarrassing. Frank, apparently, approved, and when she told him the group was spending a weekend away, he told her not to worry. She must go and he would look after us.

He spoilt us. We went to the cinema in the afternoon and saw a film about a boy who makes friends with a wild horse in Canada. Nana never let us eat sweets when we were out (Mother never took us to the cinema), but Frank bought us bags of popcorn, which we munched through the film. It was a relief, after Mother's recent self-conscious behaviour, to simply relax and have fun. That evening we went out to a Chinese restaurant and Frank teased us about what the different ingredients might be.

How long can I make the day last without speaking of the night? How can I speak the unspeakable? Subject – verb – object. It must be possible to say it in simple, chronological sentences. Jenny could. Jenny was better at putting things into words. I would think things and Jenny would put them into words. The first time I fell in love and found myself trying to deal with the demands of intimacy alone, I felt literally tongue-tied. When, in frustration no doubt at my bouts of silence, my boyfriend asked me the woman's question 'What are you thinking?' I wanted to say, 'Ask Jenny.' Why not use Jenny's words then? I can hear them in my head. They are stuck there like fossils.

* * *

I, we, were ten years old. Something woke me. Subject – verb – object. I felt something. Subject – verb – object. It hurt. Subject – verb. It hurt me. Subject – verb – object.

But the nouns are there, tin cans jangling in my consciousness, serrated edges, sharp enough to draw blood.

Torch.

Tongue.

Fear.

Jenny? Jenny, where are you? Why is he shining a torch? What is he doing? He's hurting me. There you are. You're in my bed, too, now. What has he done to you?

Silence.

Fear.

Pain.

When – he – had – finished – with – his – tongue – he – forced – us – to masturbate – him.

Is it rape if a man of forty puts his tongue into a ten-year-old child's vagina? I was twenty-one before I could have sex.

CHAPTER 34

He left us clinging to each other. We woke clinging to each other.

'I'm going to tell Mother,' were Jenny's first words. I said nothing.

'Pippa, we have to.' I said nothing but she answered my thoughts. 'Because if we don't, it will happen again.'

My next question froze inside me but she took control again. 'Well, if it does, then we'll run away.'

'He won't come in now.'

'We can't stay here like this.'

Throughout the conversation, I said nothing.

I don't know where the ten-year-old strength in Jenny came from, but it was enough for both of us. If enough means that we were able to get up and wash and dress, and pretend that nothing had changed. If enough means that, when Mother returned, we watched Frank hug her and kiss her as if everything were perfectly normal.

'The girls aren't feeling very well. I think they may have a bout of flu or something coming on.'

'They look awful! Are you alright, girls?'

'We're fine. We just had a bad night.' Jenny spoke. I couldn't look at any of them.

Mother noticed nothing. That week, we asked if we could have a television in our room and before Mother could open her mouth Frank offered to buy us one. This gave us the alibi we needed, and we retreated into each other's safety.

One night, on her return from a cheese-stealing foray, Jenny reported a conversation overheard in the living room.

'Don't you think the girls are behaving strangely at the moment?' Mother was asking Frank. 'They seem to have cut themselves off from both of us.'

'Honey, don't fret. They're probably just going through one of those bonding phases twins have. In a few years they'll be dyeing their hair different colours and fighting over the same boyfriend, so make the most of it!'

'Why don't you come to my therapy group, Frank? You take things so much in your stride.'

'So why go to therapy?' Laughing and muffled kissing sounds.

Then Mother again. 'But maybe the girls are feeling jealous. I mean, there's never been a father in their lives, and then Nana leaving, and you and I so close.'

'You could be right. They have been a little distant lately. And they did seem to resent it when you went away that weekend.'

Mother sighing.

'Listen Honey, don't be too hard on yourself. They'll be fine, trust me. Just give them time.'

'Thank you, Frank. Thank you for caring.'

* * *

Years later, when she was old enough to dramatise the past, Jenny would say that this conversation sealed the fate of men in her life. It was a good line and she threw it at men like bait. Without fail they would bite, strive to convince her that not all men were the same, peacock in front of her as the exception that would prove her rule, but no one was allowed to break the rule, and in Jenny's book all men were fair game.

It takes time for a child to learn that an adult can be gullible. I had only Jenny's version of the conversation, yet my reaction was equally raw and, whereas Jenny hatched fanciful plans to slip poison into Frank's drink, I focused on Mother's stupidity. Why can't she see? Why can't she see he doesn't love her? Why can't she see who he is? I told you he had bad eyes.

'We have to tell her,' said Jenny one day in the middle of watching *Blue Peter*.

I froze and then slowly shook my head. 'Why?'

'Because.'

'He might kill us.'

'Scaredy-cat.'

'What if he kills Mother?'

'If you don't want to I'll do it without you.'

So we did. We waited until business took Frank away to London for a weekend and we told Mother. Or rather Jenny told Mother, in words that I cannot remember, in words that Mother did not understand, did not want to understand, could not allow herself to understand, and finally understood, while I stared into a plate of shepherd's pie and discovered whole planets in it; planets which were suddenly bombarded by pieces of broken china, smashed plates, screaming, tears and confusion. I sensed rather than saw the movement around me, somehow heard my name in the screams.

'PIPPA! Is this true? Are you saying this is true?' I must have given some form of response. 'NO!'

I watched more of my planet spilling onto the table. She fled from the room and Jenny and I clung to each other.

CHAPTER 35

Then Mother made a choice. Who knows how difficult it was for her or at what level of her subconscious she processed the information she had been given by her ten-year-old daughters. What does anyone do with information like that? The man you love, the man who saved you from the precipice, the man who cares – this man you trust is supposed to have abused your daughters? God knows her relationship with the twins had never been easy. She had felt excluded from the start and their olive complexions were a constant reminder of the man who had walked out of their lives before they were born. Therapy had opened up the wounds and laid bare her resentment; she had confronted it, weeping, in a fierce and angry role-play. The twins seemed to have created their own world, a world that Nana had perhaps been able to penetrate, but which she had not. Since Nana had left they were still more distant, more moody, yet they had seemed to warm to Frank. Could they be punishing him? Punishing her? Their imaginations often frightened her. There was something too creative, too morbid, in the games they played together.

At least those are the kind of thoughts I imagine hovered over the abyss around the choice she faced. Because, at some level, however unconscious, it *was* a choice, a choice I have tried and failed to forgive, a choice that turned something in Jenny into stone. Mother made her choice. She rejected the information we had given her.

It took her twenty-four hours. Sometimes, still, when I want to understand, I try and imagine what she must have gone through to make her capable of closing her eyes; the demons that must have thrashed that night as she drank herself into temporary oblivion while her daughters retreated to their room to deal with their confusion and their fear as best they could. During the course of the night we heard sobbing, we heard music, we heard hysterical laughter, we heard a sound like broken glass and we wished for Nana. Silence finally told us that Mother's 'mood' had passed. She would sleep late into the next morning and ask us, sheepishly, whether we had made our own breakfast.

But the next morning, Jenny woke me.

'Mother's not here. She's left us a note. It says we are to make our own breakfast and watch TV, and that Mrs Hoyes will pop round to make us lunch. She says she will be back late afternoon.'

Later, much later, when we tried to piece together what happened into some kind of explanation, we decided that Mother must have made contact with Frank and arranged to meet him for lunch. She must surely have told him what we had said, must surely have confronted him and must have accepted his denial, his reassurances, his devious sympathy. How can he have dealt with her accusations and her doubts? What stuff inside his make-up allowed, enabled him to deceive the mother of the daughters he had abused? I picture his eyes and I shudder.

Then, we did not really question where she was. We ate breakfast in a daze. I was angry with Jenny. She was the one who had insisted on telling. I knew it was better to pretend it hadn't happened. I knew no good would come of telling.

'I told you, Jenny,' I accused her, coldly.

'No, you didn't.'

'I did so!'

'Didn't.'

'Did.'

'Didn't.'

'Did.'

'Did.'

'Didn't.'

'Ha, see!' She always had the last word.

'Anyway, she'll come back and say she's sorry, you just wait.'

Was she trying to convince me or herself?

Mrs Hoyes bustled in from next door, telling us not to worry, that everything would be fine. Jenny and I stared at each other, feeling naked. Was this what 'telling' meant. Would everyone know at school? Would Mr Jackson know at the post office? Of course, Mother had concocted some quite different story for our neighbour about Frank having a stroke, but in her careless and probably not very lucid haste, she had failed to tell us this. We learnt in that moment, under the magnifying glass of Mrs Hoyes' sympathy, the feeling of guilt that the victim suffers, the feeling that you are somehow sullied –and implicated – in what has been done to you by another human being.

Mother finally returned, and there was something hard in her face. There were no embraces, no tears, no soothing pats of reassurance and comfort. She sat us down and seemed to look through us.

'Now listen very carefully, girls. I know things have been difficult for you. I know I haven't been a very good mother to you in lots of ways. I know you miss Nana. Pippa, sweetheart, try not to cry. We have to speak about this.'

I couldn't help the tears. I could feel myself shaking. I willed her to hold me, but it was Jenny who took my hand. She looked straight ahead and sat totally still, and it struck me through my tears that she looked a little like Mother. We had always assumed, because Mother had told us so, that it was our mysterious father we both resembled. I looked up and saw the tears in Mother's own eyes.

'You have never had a father around and I know that I've always said your father was evil. That's because he did a very bad thing. He walked out on me the day he discovered I was pregnant. We had been married for less than a year, but he was a child – a sick, rich, spoilt child who ran back to Greece the moment the word marriage turned into something real.' She paused and sucked on her cigarette. 'But sweethearts, not all men are bad. I know it can't have been easy for you with Frank. You have no concept of what a father figure is and you see us together and you miss Nana and you feel threatened. You feel isolated.'

Perhaps Mother had been at one of her dramatherapy sessions. I squirmed with embarrassment. I looked at Jenny, but I couldn't penetrate her thoughts. I kicked her under the kitchen table, but she simply squeezed my hand and stared. What made her so 'adult' all of a sudden? I withdrew my hand. Did we have to grow up now and start going to dramatherapy like Mother? Were we going to have to 'confront our demons'? When I was little I used to imagine a witch lived under my bed and that witch had a cauldron in which she cooked a broth of snakes and spiders and unsuspecting children's feet. I was always nervous about getting up and putting my legs on the floor at night. Now I imagined 'confronting my demons' and looking into the witch's broth to see Frank's eyes swimming at the surface.

I realised that Mother was still speaking. I had drifted off, as I often did at school, as I often did in the company of adults.

'But what you did was a very bad thing, a very bad thing indeed.'

What thing? What was she talking about? I looked at the wall of Jenny's face.

'Maybe you didn't do this on purpose. Maybe you're too young to know the damage you've done. Maybe you had a nightmare or something and got confused. I don't know where you learnt about these things. Yes, they do happen, but not here, not in our house, sweethearts. I know you were angry with me for going away. I know you resent Frank for coming into our lives. Sometimes I think you blame him for Nana leaving, but it was nothing to do with Frank. If you don't know that now you will realise it one day.'

What was she talking about?

'To be honest, I don't know whether you just imagined this or whether you made it up, but I do know one thing: it didn't happen. We will never speak about it again. It didn't happen.'

It didn't happen. You see, that's what you get for telling. It didn't happen.

CHAPTER 36

Of all the institutions mankind has created, two of the most dangerous are prisons and single-sex boarding schools. Both serve a similar purpose: one saves society from having to deal with the criminals it has produced; the other saves parents from having to deal with the children they have produced. One turns delinquents into criminals; the other turns emotionally deprived children into emotionally depraved adults. Well, that was Jenny's take on it anyway.

Mother's solution, the solution that would enable her to live the lie, was to send us to boarding school. Frank was supportive; he paid the fees. Was this guilt? Or just a price worth paying? I was wrong to think that he didn't love Mother. He must have loved her to stay with her after what he did. Unless he was so sick that the fact she was our mother gave him a thrill.

Boarding school concealed everything that was abnormal in our life and heightened it by turns. Term time established us as equals among peers, removed alike from parents and the context of family, all subject to the same rules and routines. But half-terms and visiting days stranded us, along with the occasional overseas student from

Nigeria, in the care of a skeleton staff, while the majority returned to their homes or enjoyed lavish days out with smiling mothers and fathers and younger brothers and sisters. Holiday breaks meant enforced reunions with Mother and Frank, when we carefully avoided one-to-one or two- to-one contact with Frank. And something – perhaps subconscious – stopped Mother from leaving us in the house alone with him.

But boarding school did something else to make us feel abnormal. It tried to separate us. It put us into different classes, different dormitories, different activity groups. My reaction was physical: I could not eat. Jenny's was wilful: she would not eat. The result was that, as usual, we were treated the same way and punished for being difficult. We were given detentions and lines, we lost weight, we found ways and places to meet like lovers, we shunned authority and those who tried to be friendly, and we wrote long letters to Nana which were never sent.

I was described in school reports as sullen, Jenny as defiant. The other kids called us the twin twiggies, because we were so thin. There were phone calls from the headmistress to Mother, an impassioned visit by Mother pleading with us to behave, visits by a child psychologist. We resorted to fantasy, invented personas for our father and memories that never happened. He would arrive one day, our knight in shining armour, and whisk us away to a land where unicorns roamed the streets.

We never spoke about 'the thing'. One afternoon, alone in a patch of bracken and woodland that lay within the school grounds, we invented a ritual to cleanse ourselves. We wrote Frank's name on a piece of paper, folded it inside an empty matchbox and ceremoniously burned the memory, agreeing then that we would never tell anyone again. The burning part was Jenny's idea, but I made her agree to the not telling any more.

Then, two weeks after our eleventh birthday we, or rather I, met Mrs Forster. It was part of a community awareness initiative to send pupils out on home visits to a number of carefully selected old ladies, living locally and dependent on a range of home-help services to fend off the moment they would need to move into the institutionalised solitude of an old people's home. It was decided that each term one class would take part in the scheme, which meant that everyone in that class was allocated a person whom they would visit once a week for an hour instead of their homework session. My class was the first.

Mrs Forster was small and wiry and the first time I met her I thought she might break while she made me tea. She had bad arthritis and used a weird kind of pulley system to get upstairs. Her face made me want to iron it. I sat in front of her, glum and silent and embarrassed.

'Now what does a bright young thing of your age want to be doing with an old thing like me?' she laughed as she poured tea unsteadily into china cups, which looked like part of a doll's set. 'The things people think of nowadays! Why, when I was your age I would be running round outside, not forced to go and have tea with old ladies.'

'You've got a very nice house,' I volunteered, in an attempt to stop her saying what I was thinking.

'Do you think so? Well now, why don't you have a look round and tell me what you like about it.'

I shuffled off and wandered from room to room, taking in, with real curiosity, the photos that lined whole shelves and mantelpieces.

'So what do you think?' she asked the moment I had returned.

'I think you've got a lot of photos,' I said, and she smiled.

Over the coming weeks, I learnt to respect the lines in her face, some of them the signs of too much Indian sunshine in her youth, and I learnt that wrinkles tell a story. I learnt to see in the ridges around her mouth and the sharp crow's feet at the corner of her eyes the havoc that laughter had wreaked in her lifetime. Each week she told me more about her life, more about the photos that crowded her house and her mind, and I found myself truly relaxing in adult company for the first time since Nana.

And, without knowing why, I didn't tell her that I had a sister. I suppose, looking back, that her home was a haven from everything else in my life, everything that made me 'me' – and Jenny was part of that. For the first time, something in me yearned for a space of my own.

'Let me go in your place next time.' Jenny interrupted my thoughts one morning break.

'It wouldn't work. She would know it was you.'

'But you haven't told her about me. How would she know you had a sister?'

I was sure that I hadn't mentioned this to Jenny, yet there were no secrets between us. I resisted, but she was forceful and, feeling obscurely guilty, I finally gave in.

'Don't talk too much, just sit and listen,' I coached Jenny, in preparation for the visit. 'Ask her about the photo on the right of the bookshelf. We haven't done that one yet.'

And I tied my hair up like Jenny usually did and examined myself in the mirror, wondering nervously if I would get away with replacing Jenny in her homework session, while she had tea with Mrs Forster.

No one noticed that it was me at the homework session and, when I went to Mrs Forster the following week, she said nothing to indicate that she had noticed anything strange.

'Mrs Forster, do you have good eyesight?' I asked her over tea.

'Why, I didn't need these until I was seventy-five!' she chirped, removing her glasses and looking straight at me.

I glanced down, swallowing an unknown sense of disappointment.

The next visit to Mrs Forster was supposed to be the last, and I felt physically heavy. She was as cheerful as ever and I resented her for it.

'Oh, by the way, Pippa, I hope you don't mind, but I had a word with your headmistress, Mrs Hawkins, and she has agreed to let you keep coming for tea if you want to.'

'Really?' I laughed. I sounded like Jenny.

'Oh, and one more thing, young lady, I think you have a little confession to make, don't you?'

'What do you mean?' I floundered, embarrassed, realising she had known all along that it wasn't me the day Jenny had come in my place.

'That was a mean trick to play on an old lady!'

'Oh Mrs Forster, I didn't mean . . .'

But her eyes were twinkling and my heart was racing with joy.

CHAPTER 37

As we got older, Jenny's tangles with authority gathered momentum. We had changed schools, moving not more than a few miles to a private girls' school as mediocre as the prep school we left behind us. When Jenny misbehaved I was no longer automatically drawn in by association and, very slowly, we created different allegiances at school and people stopped referring to us constantly as 'the twins'. Yet our friendships with other people continued to be superficial. Jenny was fickle, enjoying an audience and easily getting bored, while I discovered an interest in reading and study, which earned me a reputation as 'the boring one'. And Frank was right. Jenny seized the first opportunity she could to dye her hair a different colour, although we never fought over the same boyfriend.

Having smoked her first cigarette at the age of thirteen behind the sports hall in front of an admiring audience, at fourteen Jenny dyed her hair pink and converted this into a political statement in the face of resistance by the headmistress. She was antagonistic, asserting her refusal to conform through the addition of pink accessories to her school uniform: a scarf, a badge, a pair of tights.

She challenged the English teacher's assertion that no one was 'obliged' to read aloud from Shakespeare by persuading every single one of the class to decline when their turn came round. She refused to sing at assemblies on the grounds that 'God couldn't exist, else he wouldn't allow children to be raped.'

But there was a problem. She didn't have a boyfriend, and to be truly rebellious at that age you needed a boyfriend – and you needed to do things with him (things which we had known about since the age of eight and experienced at the age of ten).

Boys were a different species. We didn't have brothers to go home to, brothers who brought friends back and played hide and seek and sardines in the dark. Boys were supposed to be tall and handsome and good at kissing. We had no idea how to actually talk to them.

The difference between Jenny and me was that I simply wasn't interested, while Jenny was greedy for experience.

'I am going to lose my virginity before the summer,' she told me in January, just like that.

'But you haven't even got a boyfriend and if you had one, you might not want to sleep with him,' I pleaded.

'You know what your problem is? You've got too many hang-ups.'

'I've got too many hang-ups! Who's got the obsession with losing her virginity?'

'Oh fuck off, Pippa. No one's asking you to drop your prissy little knickers.'

'So who exactly is going to be the lucky man?' I jeered.

'Samantha's brother.'

'You mean George? But he must be about four years older than us, and anyway you don't even like Samantha. How are you going to get George interested in you?'

George was Samantha's main source of popularity. He was the stuff of girly fantasies about chancing to pass beneath the mistletoe . . . and he sometimes came to collect Samantha at weekends.

'You watch me.'

Where did her confidence come from? It took me years to realise it was a form of anger.

Jenny found out as much as she could about George from Samantha. She learnt that he had recently split up with his girlfriend, had passed his driving test and had been given a car by his parents, so she simply sent him a Valentine's card. She showed it to me in anticipated triumph. 'I would love a ride in your car. You won't regret it.' She included details of how to contact her and it worked. She had sex with him on their third outing, and if he boasted to his mates that he had slept with a virgin from the local girls' school, he had no idea that she had planned it all.

CHAPTER 38

While Jenny experimented with make-up and the male psyche, I swotted. I got nine GCSEs to Jenny's six and I spent hours deliberating over my choice of A-levels, while Jenny simply opted for what she thought would give her an easy ride. Both of us chose Spanish, perhaps in unspoken loyalty to the memory of Nana (we learnt that she had died of a stroke in a rare letter from Mother), but I agonised for days over the other two, aware, unlike most of my peers and certainly my sister, that I was shaping the options for my degree, which would shape the rest of my life. My love of reading competed with the allure of subjects like zoology or social anthropology. In the end, I opted for Spanish, French and English literature. Ironically, Jenny's choice was not very different from mine. She chose Spanish, English literature and drama.

Jenny protected me from the demands of peer pressure and social convention. Through her I had just enough contact with boys and friends at school to ensure that words like 'weird' or 'frigid' were held at bay. Some of her vivacity rubbed off on me and distracted attention from my own awkwardness. Sometimes I resented her, felt jealous of friendships that excluded me. Yet mostly I was grateful to have her as a buffer between me and direct experience. While she buried childhood abuse under as many new pieces of male anatomy as possible, I discovered my own sexual urges slowly, on paper, as I ploughed through Jane Austen and D.H. Lawrence.

'You can't go on intellectualising sex, Pips. You'll have to join the real world one day, you know.' Jenny was lying on her back, chewing a piece of grass and looking up at the hazy English summer sky. She looked peaceful – deceptively peaceful.

'But I want it to mean something. I want it to be part of a relationship with a future, and I'm not ready for that, so I'm not ready for the sex part either.'

'Pips, do you disapprove of me?' It was supposed to be a throwaway question but it was too self-consciously so.

'Jens, you're a different person. What you do is what you do and I respect your choices.'

'But you disapprove. You think I'm a slut.' She was crying now, but I couldn't lie to her, couldn't hide the fact that I never understood – until years later – how she could give herself so carelessly.

'Don't you think I feel disgusted at myself? Don't you think I envy you and wish I was like you? But I have to live and I don't want to live in a cage. I'm not like you. I can't live through books. I need real life.'

Her words stung at one level, but they were also a revelation. I had not realised how much she needed my approval or how much self-hatred lay beneath the brash confidence that made her so attractive.

'Jenny, I don't blame you. Maybe we both need to learn from each other.'

* * *

That summer, the summer we were seventeen, we drew up a list of goals. Like the burning of the matchbox years previously, it was ritualistic, each of us committing to paper our own aspirations in private, and then sharing and stapling our pieces of paper together for posterity. We allowed ourselves five goals.

Pippa
1   *I will get good A-level grades and I will get into a good university and get a good degree.*
2   *I will try and be more open to the people around me.*
3   *I will lose my virginity with someone who cares for me (but I will not get too hung up about this and will not pin too many hopes on it).*
4   *I will never take Jenny for granted.*
5   *I will do something worthwhile with my life.*

Jenny
1   *I will travel and see the world.*
2   *I will try and learn to concentrate on study and becoming a better person.*
3   *I will never be owned.*
4   *I will meet someone one day who I will want to remain faithful to forever.*
5   *I will always be there for Pips.*

* * *

I think, now, of those goals and the young minds that set them, and I wish there was a way back into the past, a way to make all of them come true.

CHAPTER 39

The end of school for Jenny was a window she looked through every day, a window she longed to open and climb through. I had agreed, with some misgivings, to her plan to spend a year travelling together before going to university. How would we manage? What would we live on? Where would we go? Would Mother agree?

'Fuck Mother, Pips. Don't you realise we don't have to do what she wants anymore? From now on decisions belong to us!'

The summer after our exams was the last summer we spent at 'home'. Jenny paraded her latest Queen-loving, leather-trousered, biker-boyfriend like a piece of junk jewellery for everyone to disapprove of, and made snide remarks to Frank on the rare occasions we all sat round the same table. I remember the first day she brought Gary back to 'meet the family'. She arrived triumphantly late for the Italian meal Mother had prepared.

'Oh, I'm so sorry we're late Mother. We didn't realise what time it was, did we Gary?' Winking at Gary and shooting a glance at Frank. 'Gary, this is my mother and this is not my father.' She paused for dramatic effect. 'His name is Frank, rhymes with –'

'Jenny, that's enough! Do have a seat, Gary.' Poor Mother. 'Let me pour you some wine.'

'So Gary, now you know all about me,' offered Frank, feigning amusement, or perhaps genuinely amused, 'let's hear about you. What do you want to do with your life?'

'He plays the guitar, and he rides a motorbike and me!' The look on Jenny's face was vicious. 'He's a great shag!' There followed a kind of collective splutter as Mother coughed, Frank cleared his throat and poor Gary, who had not yet opened his mouth, almost choked on his wine. We hadn't even started the spaghetti. I looked at Jenny and pleaded restraint with my eyes. How many times have I looked at her the same way since?

With the months of concentration for A-levels behind me, I became acutely aware of my own social clumsiness and even yielded to Jenny's attempts to instil some sense of fashion in me. I went out on a rare date with the brother of a friend, wearing a short black dress, which made Frank do a double take. I blushed with an emotion that felt alien to me. It was a feeling of both power and anger, a shot of adrenaline, which persuaded me to join Jenny in her resolve to leave 'home' as soon as possible.

When I learnt that I had got three As, my delight was tempered by a sense of guilt that I had done so much better than Jenny, but she was sweetly generous, proclaiming louder than anyone that she was proud of her sister's achievement and whispering mischievously that she had all the As when it came to orgasms, so it was only fair.

A door opened, which neither I nor my teachers had anticipated: the opportunity to sit for Oxbridge, the chance to turn another of the five goals into reality. Jenny was amazingly supportive, and tackled the practicalities and her own disappointment about the delay this meant to our travels with quiet determination. Adamant about leaving home, we rented a student flat and she temped to pay the bills and support me while I prepared for more exams. I knew that this was a sacrifice; I knew that she was putting one of her own goals on hold for me.

The day I was accepted at Oxford brought with it a strange mixture of elation and fear; hysterical laughter, which turned to tears with the sudden knowledge of what this meant. The beginning of the unknown in a way that nothing had ever been truly unknown; the first step into a life on my own, without Jenny by my side.

'Don't be daft, Pips. I'm only going to be in London. We'll see each other all the time.' She had a place to study drama at Goldsmiths. 'And anyway we don't even need to think about all that stuff until October. We've got six months of the world ahead of us!' She protected me like a much older sister, yet she was only seven minutes older.

* * *

Before we left on our travels, I had tea with Mrs Forster, fearful that this time might be the last. She had turned ninety that year and still managed at home – just. Each year she seemed to grow smaller and drier, like a prune in a desert, but her eyes were still sharp and she still knew the story behind every photo in her house. This time I took her a photo, a picture taken on the day we celebrated my acceptance at Oxford. Unaware that a photo was being taken, my face was partially covered by hair blowing across it and my smile was unusually confident. Mrs Forster beamed and insisted that I put the photo in pride of place in the centre of the mantelpiece.

'Now, my poppet, if you're going to be wandering round the world looking for trouble, you must have a picture of mine, too. Which one will you have?'

'Goodness, I don't know. Which one do you want me to have?'

'Whichever one you want. Now go and choose.'

I chose a picture of her as a young woman, having tea in India. She stood on a lawn, against a backdrop of rampant flowers, holding a cup of tea in one hand and a parasol in the other. She must have been talking to someone outside the frame; her eyes glanced past the camera lens and her face was laughing. She was beautiful. I could only just see this woman in the little old lady before me, but I recognised her spirit. This was how I wanted to remember her.

'Ah yes,' she sighed, as I tentatively showed her the picture I had chosen. 'Robert was the man I was talking to, a charming man. Perhaps we will meet again in the next life.'

And so at last, armed with a photo of Nana, a photo of Mrs Forster and a photo of us, I climbed, just behind my sister, through the window that had beckoned to Jenny for so long.

CHAPTER 40

I still have our diaries from the six months we spent, flirting with danger, hitch-hiking around Europe, believing ourselves invincible and oh-so grown-up. They read very differently. Mine is self-consciously observant, recording facts and conversations with an anthropological curiosity. The 'me' in that world is passive, revealed occasionally by reactions to events or people, but never openly introspective. Things happened, or didn't happen, which I know were important to me then and which I remember clearly now, yet for all its meticulous attention to detail, my diary is silent. The world is a succession of encounters between two pronouns: 'we' and 'they'. There is a sort of dreaminess about it, a shy account of a journey, full of speculation about others.

Jenny's diary is fiercely honest and introspective. The encounters, which for me are recorded as the essence of experience, are, for Jenny, springboards for stream-of-consciousness rants about her own identity and place in the world. I blush when I read them, embarrassed equally by their naïve, self-important content and by the blatant lack of shame in them. I was shocked to discover, when I read her diary for the first time, that the 'no telling' we had agreed to over the ritualistic burning of the matchbox with Frank's name in it was no more than a concession to the outside world. Because I had buried the memory so deeply, because we never spoke about it, because I would not have dreamed of referring to it in my diary, I assumed that Jenny, too, had packed this away in a forbidden part of her consciousness.

Jenny ate experience; I looked at it. Yet there was a strength in being together that gave me a kind of mute confidence. We were noticed wherever we went. On a hippy beach in Crete, I caught myself for the first time not wanting to look away as my eyes met those of a tall, blond, twenty-something Dutchman on the other side of the campfire flames. Jenny noticed, too, and sidled up to me with a joint in her hand.

'Here, have some Dutch courage,' she giggled. 'Go get him, sis!'

He must have sensed my inexperience. Over the next few nights we walked along the beach, we bathed in the moonlight, we kissed in warm water. I laughed at the memory of my sister when she first discovered an interest in boys, practising French kisses on a pillow, and relaxed under the supervision of desire. Every muscle in my body ached for this Dutchman and, at last, one soft summer evening in the sand, I watched him put on a condom and gently, oh so gently, caress my wetness to keep me ready for him. I closed my eyes and then I felt something pushing at me and my insides froze. I lurched away from him and cried with incomprehension. He was kind. 'The first time is always hard,' he said gently. I know, I know, I thought . . . He will never know how grateful I was that he did not try again.

To an extent, Jenny and I switched roles, with me playing elder sister. It was shyness that did this really. My shyness about losing myself, my fear of losing control, meant that I watched out for both of us. Where Jenny's greed for direct experience meant that she would lose contact with reality under the influence of drugs or alcohol, I stayed anchored and gently watchful. I envied her ability to let go, yet it frightened me.

Our worst arguments were when she disappeared without telling me where she was going. I worried myself sick one night when she didn't come 'home' to our tent. Still angry with her two days later, I made the mistake of reading what she'd put in her diary after that night.

I need to feel free. Why can't she understand that? I don't want my life to be mapped out in predictable reactions and patterns. Sometimes she makes me feel trapped, like an alter ego looking over my shoulder, tut-tutting about what I do and say. I don't want to be judged all the time. I don't want to live a life with no risks, no spontaneity. She doesn't understand that I don't have the same needs as her. She's so rational and intellectual about everything. I want to feel, I want to live, I want to experiment. So what if I have sex with someone I'll never see again? I didn't even know his name and he's leaving tomorrow, but that was the whole appeal. He made me feel free. He wanted to take my address, but I disappeared while he was having a pee and he didn't know where I'd come from. Why can't she see there is nothing wrong with that? Why can't she just leave me alone?

* * *

Even twin sisters shouldn't read each other's diaries.

'We could try and find him,' I mused, as we sat in a taverna with our daily ration of Greek salad and spaghetti.

'What for?' She sliced viciously into a piece of tomato. 'He's bound to be an arsehole. Who wants to meet a father who left them before they were born? I bet he's some swanky financial advisor who gets off on persuading old ladies to give him a big cut when they die and they go to their deathbeds grateful that such a charming man has helped them secure their kids' future.'

'Maybe, maybe not. What if we're wrong? What do we know except what Mother told us, and she's hardly the most reliable person in the world? Maybe he left her before he knew she was pregnant. Maybe he would like to see us.' Inwardly, I tried to conjure up what he would look like, the look of disbelief and tenderness on his face when we told him who we were.

'Dream, dream, dream,' sang Jenny into my thoughts, and I laughed with her.

'Perhaps you're right. Anyway, how would we find him?' I couldn't let it go completely.

'We won't. At least I never will.'

'I don't suppose I ever will either.'

'So where shall we go next? Don't you think we've been here long enough?'

Ever restless, ever greedy for more.

I wandered through a mental gallery of films: *Midnight Express, Last Tango in Paris, A Room with a View*.

'How about Florence?'

CHAPTER 41

I got my first grey hair when I was twenty. The most appalling thing about it was that it was a pubic hair. Jenny laughed and laughed when I told her.

'I'm sorry, Pips,' she choked. 'It's just too ironic!'

'Yeah, yeah, I know,' I giggled, despite a twinge somewhere inside. 'A virgin with grey pubes. Just my luck!'

I singled it out with great care and cut it off at the root with a pair of nail scissors, but my pruning only served to make it stronger and longer when it grew back. To this day, I still go through the pruning ritual, and to this day it remains my only grey pube, a rogue reminder of destiny.

Oxford made me feel much smaller than hitching round Europe had done. The smallest bit was my tongue. As if there was a faulty connection somewhere in the plumbing between my brain and speech faculties. I didn't think that I was nervous or shy in the conventional sense, I simply couldn't think of anything to contribute to the soup of conversation around me. I had always assumed that the drive in me to do well at exams meant that I was competitive, yet I recoiled from the competitive banter of fresh undergraduates staking out new friendships. When I did think of something to say, I sounded like a bad actress, the timing somehow never quite right. I laughed when no one else did and was silent when I should have been laughing. I became aware of a hint of embarrassment in the way that people looked at me. This was new. This was part of my new life, part of life without the protection of Jenny.

New faces meant a barrage of what Jenny and I called 'search questions'. Where are you from? Did you take a year out? What are you reading? What A-levels did you do? Have you got a boyfriend?

Jenny had me in fits when we met in London at the end of the first week, reeling off daft answers in silly accents.

'The moon . . . Yeah, I took one to the cinema, but he was as dull as a cow's bottom . . . Tristram Shandy, my dear . . . Cave psychology, bark painting and the history of pornography. And you? . . . No, have you got a sock?'

But the problem was that when people started asking about me, I either answered with 'we' and then found that they assumed I had a permanent boyfriend in tow or I started to tell them about Jenny and found that they looked uncomfortable. Didn't anyone else have brothers and sisters? I asked Jenny if the same thing happened to her.

'Yeah, it's a great way to get men interested! You talk about "the times we had on the road" and they think either "Wow, she must be up for it if she's been hitching round Europe with a bloke" or "Wow, she's got a boyfriend, but let's see if I can rise to the challenge and get into her knickers." Either way you come out way more interesting than the girl next door!'

I laughed, but went quiet.

'Don't worry, Pips, it'll get better, you know.' She was big sister again.

One day when I was staring at the mole on someone's cheek, it dawned on me that there was something wrong in my eye contact with people. The realisation was fatal. The harder I tried, the more difficult it was to look into people's eyes when they were talking, and the more I tried to look into their eyes and not at their eyebrows or a pimple on their chin, the more difficult it was to concentrate on what they were saying, and therefore the more difficult it was to think of anything to say in the expectant gaps at the end of their sentences – and on and on until I became quite dizzy with the effort of simple conversation.

Books, on the other hand, were less demanding. They were happy for your eyes to drift over them, line after line, page after page, at your own pace, unchallenged. The college library still harboured the risk of unwanted eye contact with students who recognised you and tried to start a conversation, but the Radcliffe Camera became my personal haven. I took Jenny inside once and she wanted to leave immediately. But I loved the gloom and the high ceilings, the echo of a pencil accidentally dropped, the sheer aura of academia. I revelled in the literary labyrinths of Borges, sensitive to the surrealism of his stories, oblivious to any political context. I highlighted the quirks of Gabriel Garcia Marquez that made me laugh out loud, although my essay on his magic realism left my tutor slightly bemused. I lapped up the darkness of Baudelaire's poetry and forged my own brand of literary criticism. I started to wear glasses, but not for reading. I needed them for the outside, for conversation.

CHAPTER 42

The university calendar turned life into a sequence of chapters in a way that the repetitiveness of the school year had never achieved. Perhaps it was our age, perhaps it was the amount I was reading, perhaps it was the insularity of undergraduate life at Oxford, but the four years sit in my memory like a book neatly parcelled into chapters.

Chapter one: Weekends spent mostly in London with Jenny. Easier to spend time with her there than for her to come here. Only friends here are books.

Chapter two: Prolonged affair between Jenny and Daniel. First time she has ever used word 'boyfriend'. Discovered Borges. Started wearing glasses.

Chapter six . . . Jenny always used to say that there are fewer surprises in life than you think; that the causal links are there in our lifestyles and our choices. If you have a habit of clubbing and no fear of sex on the first night, you are more likely to meet a fucked-up paramedic turning to drink to help him bring back the dead. If you wear red power suits and matching lipstick to work, you are more likely to break up someone else's marriage than if you rely on Dateline to meet the man of your dreams.

If you are a twenty-year-old virgin bookworm at Oxford University, you are more likely to meet someone in a library than outside it. And if you meet someone in a library at the age of twenty, he is more likely to have a bespectacled, rather nervous, laconic, slightly clumsy sort of presence than that of a broad-shouldered, handsome stud whose main interests are surfing and skiing.

So it's no surprise that the fucked-up paramedic ends up giving you a sexually transmitted disease and a black eye. Or that the man whose marriage you have broken up later has an affair with your best friend. Or that the self-conscious bookworm, whose sex life has been confined to the four walls of his imagination, turns out to be tremendously gentle and patient in bed.

It was on the night of my twenty-first birthday that I finally lost my virginity. By then Eddie and I had spent endless hours together, feeling our way towards some kind of space that was comfortable for both of us. He was shy in public, but quirky in private, and I warmed to his gentle wit and his cautious interest in me. I began, oh-so slowly, to talk about myself. I told him about Jenny. I told him that she was prettier than me and vivacious and wacky and incapable of sitting still.

'No, she isn't,' he said to me after he met her for the first time.

'Isn't what?'

'Prettier than you.'

I looked up at him. My eyes met his through the safety of two layers of glass and didn't flinch.

Jenny was brittle at first and Eddie was careful not to say what he thought; that she was jealous, that this was probably the first time that anyone else had challenged her dominance in my life.

We read poems and discussed the echoes of books in our own young lives over languid summer afternoons in long riverside grass. I relaxed gently into sustained eye contact and a warm emotion that I had only read about. Our words were safe, our revelations partial and non-threatening. He never asked why I had lost my virginity so late or if I had had boyfriends before, and I never thought to ask him the same questions. Dear Eddie. I wonder where he is now? We drifted apart slowly in the same way that we had drifted together, with the inevitability and calmness of a tide.

CHAPTER 43

In the end, the friendships that lasted longest were the London ones, not the Oxford ones. That was the way we referred to them. Do you remember the London crowd? Janet and her ability to put her foot into everything she encountered; Jamie and his ambition to become a rock star – or a politician; Will and his closet gay mannerisms that fooled no one; Sarah and her maternal urge to save anything, from whales to the man next door. What sound bites would they have chosen for us? Jenny and her lust for life and limb, Pippa and her . . .?

Spain was a long chapter. We were reunited in Granada for our 'year abroad'. We rented a tiny third-floor flat, attended the university intermittently and basked in the luxury of our college grants.

There were flashpoints. I lashed out at Jenny in a way that surprised both of us. She grew impatient with my continued commitment to reading and what she called my 'lack of adventure'. Her own enthusiasm for adventure resulted in a near-death collision on the back of a moped at five in the morning on a winding mountain road, clinging onto a drunken shepherd she had picked up in a village disco.

'What the fuck were you playing at?' I asked once relief had subsided.

'What the fuck would you know?' She knew exactly where to hurt. Later, she cried in my arms. 'I'm sorry, Pips, you know I don't mean it.'

We invented a game called Life on the Back of a Cigarette Packet. You played it in restaurants or bars, in the Alhambra or on the beach – anywhere with lots of people. When it was your turn you chose a person or a couple, without saying who they were, and you described their lives or their characters. The other person had to guess who you were talking about.

It was my turn. 'He and his wife are divorced and this is his weekend with the children. He always takes them out, because it's easier if they're outside. He can't help thinking about the fact that they know the man who took his wife away better than their father. It kills him. It makes him awkward in their presence. After he has returned them, he goes out and gets drunk. He might even sleep with a prostitute, and then he'll feel really bad, because that was what started it all; that was when she left him. What he doesn't know is that one of the kids isn't his anyway. The little girl that reminds him of himself when he was little isn't his child. Only his ex-wife knows that.'

Jenny was laughing. 'I thought I was the one with the morbid imagination! Those three, eating ice-creams and hardly speaking!'

'Yep. Go on then, your turn.'

'She is with her best friend. She feels as if she has known her forever and she would do anything for her.'

I glanced around the gardens, which were swarming with people, looking in vain for the giveaway clue of two girls together. I looked at Jenny's face. She seemed to be looking nowhere.

'But sometimes she feels that there is something eating her insides, something dark and dangerous, something she can't understand, doesn't want to understand, like that feeling you get when you're somewhere very high, the temptation to jump, as if something is pulling at you.'

I looked into Jenny's face, but she seemed to see straight through me.

'It doesn't last long, but it comes back again and again, like an ulcer.'

I scanned the faces around us. I felt something like panic inside me. Then I saw them. Two girls, in their late twenties, one wearing dungarees and bright red lipstick with her hair tied up in a red ribbon, round and jolly, the other with her arm hooked through her friend's, black shorts and T-shirt, black rings around her eyes.

Today, I wonder if Jenny was trying to tell me something. Today, I believe in coincidence.

CHAPTER 44

There is a photo in the last Oxford chapter of Eddie and me. We stand in a sea of black gowns and mortarboards, looking like two awkward extras on a film set. Everyone is laughing, and bottles of champagne or cheap sparkling wine are fizzing all around like fireworks. There is a girl being transported on a hospital bed, covered in red roses and baked beans, and laughing uncontrollably. It is the last day of finals and the street is awash with the longed-for significance of this precious moment in the young, privileged lives of Oxford's students.

Eddie and I reach for each other and hug with awkward warmth. We have stopped sleeping together, but there is a tenderness still and an absence of anyone else. We are carried along by the crowd and join shyly in the night's festivities. I think of Jenny and shudder slightly to imagine the abandon with which she will surely celebrate the end of her finals next week. I am glad she is not here.

Eddie and I will not see each other again, though he will remain on my Christmas card list for years. He asks me what I am going to do. He knows that I have avoided the milk round of City interviews that even he has succumbed to. I don't know. Life stretches out in front of me like sand dunes rippling into the distance, and I wonder if I will have the energy to climb them. I feel hot and uncomfortable and trapped in the image that I have chosen. If I lie down maybe I will slowly burn into the sand.

* * *

Jenny would know what to do. I expected, relied on, her decisiveness, yet I was surprised by her single-mindedness when it came. She had it all worked out. She was going to do a PGCE and become a drama teacher. She needed something that would give her time to travel, but she didn't want the kind of suited travel that a job in the City might mean, and anyway she wouldn't be able to stand the crap that went with it. As simple as that. How I envied her certainty. How it fooled me for a while.

We moved into a flat in Brixton and my own lack of certainty filled shelf after shelf with second-hand books. I buried myself in the sand of the lives I read about and put my glasses on for the all-night parties that were an inevitable part of sharing a flat with Jenny. There was something slightly schizophrenic about it: days which made me feel real within the fingered pages of imaginary lives and nights where I blushed from the sidelines of Jenny's existence.

Once, I got up in the middle of the night for an Aspirin and found her in the kitchen with her shirt open and her legs on a man's lap, while another man was stroking her hair.

'Hey, sis come and join us.' One of the men was chopping up lines of cocaine on an old record sleeve.

I blushed and wished I had my glasses. Jenny looked at me like a dog, pleading. My heart went out to her suddenly and something in me longed to say yes, for her sake. I remembered her words at the Alhambra, but there was a knot inside me that resisted and silence swallowed my resolve.

* * *

A coincidence rescued me from the pressure building around the lack of work and direction in my life. The owner of the second-hand bookshop where I whiled away so many hours announced that he was setting up another branch in north London and needed someone to stay on and run the Brixton shop. He shocked me by asking if I would like the job.

'But I don't know anything about selling books.'

'You know more about buying books than anyone who walks in here, and your enthusiasm is infectious. You'll be good at selling them.'

My enthusiasm? It came as a shock to realise that we had established a kind of friendship and that I was sufficiently at ease in his company to discuss the books I read. Enthusiasm. I played proudly with the concept in my head and nodded my acceptance. Jenny was sensitive enough to congratulate me. I knew that something in her must have rebelled at the notion of such work, such tedium, such lack of adventure, but I rejoiced in what I had stumbled upon. And in the weeks and months to come, a kind of confidence swelled, slowly and long overdue, inside me.

The clink of the bell as the door opened to let in a customer sparked a momentary flutter of trepidation, which turned quickly to eager curiosity. I would watch as people lingered in different parts of the shop and I played mental guessing games. This one will go to the gardening section, that one will look for himself in the biography of an Antarctic explorer, she is investigating the birth of feminism.

'Can I help? Do you know what you are looking for?' I would ask softly.

'I'm not really sure . . .' This one was a woman who would have looked less out of place rock-climbing in the Lake District than she did here. I shared a spontaneous and imaginary CV with Jenny in my head. She's in her thirties, loves dogs and has just been abandoned by her husband.

'Are you looking for something for yourself or a present for someone else?' My question was safe.

'For me, actually. The thing is I'm not a great reader, but I'm going away for a bit, to East Africa, and I wanted to take something relevant.' Bloody hell, I was right, I thought! She needed change – and inspiration. I warmed to the shyness in her.

'Have you read any of Hemingway's novels?'

'Well, yes, I've read *The Green Hills of Africa*, but I was looking for something a bit more, I don't know . . .'

'Modern? Or personal?' I offered tentatively.

'It doesn't have to be modern, but, I don't know, something . . .'

'I tell you what,' I offered, 'how about *West with the Night*? Have you heard of Beryl Markham?' And when I saw her hesitate, I jumped in before she needed to answer. 'She was a fascinating woman, brought up in the Highlands of Kenya in the early 1900s. She flouted convention wherever she went and competed in a man's world as a horse trainer. Then she trained as a pilot and became the first woman to make a solo flight across the Atlantic from London to America. And then she wrote her autobiography. It's a wonderful book; intense and strangely uplifting. Not really very personal in the conventional sense, but I loved it.' I could see that she was hooked. 'And she was always surrounded by controversy. There was even a scandal about whether it was really her who wrote the book or her third husband!'

'That sounds perfect, thank you.'

'Do come back and tell me if you liked it!'

I always invited people back to give their reactions to the books I recommended, and I was always happily surprised whenever they did. The shy rock-climbing lady came back three months later. She had enjoyed the book so much she wanted to read the biographies of Beryl Markham. On her third visit to the bookshop, her first words were, 'Gosh, she really was a bit of a bitch, wasn't she?' And so, slowly, I began to form friendships that Jenny did not understand.

CHAPTER 45

'I've done it!'

'Done what?'

We were sipping *citron pressé* and dry white wine in Café Rouge. Jenny was flushed and brimming with tales of her recent trip to Sri Lanka. She had asked me to go with her, but I had declined, partly through a genuine lack of available holiday and partly, guiltily, through weariness, the weariness of bearing witness to Jenny's excesses.

'You should do a trip you know, Pips. I mean a trip on your own. It's so fulfilling. I was scared shitless at first –'

'You were?' I laughed.

'Yes, actually, I was, but then you discover things about yourself that you had no idea were even there. I can't explain it really, there is something – I don't know – invigorating about being self-sufficient and making your own choices. Even the most trivial of choices – what to eat for breakfast, where to go, who to speak to. What are you laughing at?'

'You! It's so good to see you. I missed you!' We were both laughing, reunited.

'So,' I remembered, 'what is it you've done? You haven't told me yet.'

She stubbed out her cigarette, leant across the table and said in a mock stage whisper.

'I've joined the Mile-High Club!'

'Jenny, you didn't!' We were like thirteen-year-olds, giggling because we'd seen the shape of an erection in a boy's trousers. 'Who with? How? Did you –'

'Yes, of course I used a condom, Pips!'

'Well?'

'Well what?'

'Well tell me about it then!'

And she poured out the details, like an open book.

I was only vaguely aware of movement in the toing-and-froing of people around us, a warm backdrop of jazz-softened voices as we filled in the spaces that absence had created between us.

'So how are things, Pips? News on the Michael front?' Michael was a rather untypically good-looking book collector and there was the faintest hint of mutual interest, which Jenny had latched on to.

'You know there is something of the book collector's mind in you, Jenny,' I teased her.

'Fuck off!'

'No, really, your obsessiveness is like a collector's – or a trainspotter's!'

'Fuck off, Pips. Let's get another bottle of wine. Anyway, you're the one who's OCD. You treat your books like pet Labradors!'

We could never get away from the comparisons. We were like mirrors facing each other, our identities reflected again and again in images of images, disappearing into infinity. There was a remoteness in both of us, a distance from the world. For all the carnal ferocity of her attempts to devour experience, Jenny remained somehow untouched. She had her own metaphorical glasses. Sometimes I think her frustration with me was to do with her own refusal to deal in the abstract. In her mind, my books were a symbol of denial, a denial of the here and now, which lay at the core of her being. We shared a love of fantasy, yet we responded differently to it.

Jenny drifted in and out of the places she visited without any real awareness or interest in the political circumstances or history of the country. She reacted to people, not to facts, and what she brought back from her travels was something intensely personal. I *seemed* apolitical, she *was* apolitical. My own apparent reticence had more to do with my distrust of sound bites than a lack of interest in the state of the world. Maybe Jenny was right. Maybe I had my books to blame for that. I couldn't deal in the black and white of most current affairs conversations, but Jenny was the only other person I knew who couldn't read a newspaper.

Jenny returned from the loo and prodded me out of my reverie. 'Hey, Pips, wake up, you're drifting off. Time to go. I've already paid the bill.'

I was dizzy with the pale blush of white wine. I am dizzy now with memory.

CHAPTER 46

I turn a page in my mind to a time that is bittersweet. We are sitting on sequined cushions on the floor, around a table laden with pita bread and Moroccan dips, struggling to stay comfortable, but enjoying the novelty of the restaurant. I am nervous, next to Michael's brother (nothing happened with Michael, but by chance Johnny knows his brother), and Jenny is sitting opposite, next to Johnny. There are two more people, friends of Johnny's. I see the way that Johnny is looking at Jenny and I feel sad for him, protective almost, wanting to warn him. Johnny does not deserve to join the queue of men to pay the price for Jenny's past.

I divide Jenny's men into two types. There is the caricature, the macho who peacocks his charm and seduces, and who is unknowingly seduced. He brings out the sadist in Jenny, sets in motion a gentle tug of war, which she slices into before he gets around to losing interest in her. And there is the earnest type, who wants to prove that he is different. His lesson will be hardest; he will be hurt as well as humiliated.

'So are you permanently based in London now, Johnny?' This is one of his friends speaking. 'No more tin mines?' A brief aside for my benefit, 'You know that Johnny is a geologist – bit of a weirdo – used to spend weeks at a time in total isolation on rock faces or something in Bolivia.'

'Thanks for the introduction, Andy.' He laughs then, spontaneously, loudly, incongruously, and I can see everyone being drawn in. 'I still get out once in a while, but most of the time I'm office-based now.'

'You! Office-based? Poor fuckers in the office!'

'Yes, I know, it doesn't really sound like me, does it?' Johnny laughs again and I wonder why. 'So is anyone else around here office-based?'

'My sister is bookshop-based. Does that count?'

I flinch at being drawn into the spotlight, but Johnny just looks at me with a wide smile and says, 'No, that definitely doesn't count at all, and nor does your classroom, Jenny. Completely different beasts. Andy, on the other hand, is the worst kind of office junky there is.' His tone is teasing but warm, and Andy looks pleased.

And so we talk and laugh about the politics and the banter, the quirks and routines that define office life in our modern world. It occurs to me that Johnny doesn't fit either of Jenny's male stereotypes. He often and easily becomes the centre of attention, but he doesn't dominate; he doesn't litter the conversation with anecdotes or knowledge for effect. This man is no peacock, but he isn't earnest either. He laughs too much for that.

'What happens when an Australian and a Norwegian have sex?'

Oh shit, I think, a joke. Andy is warming up to his punch line. My eyes seek Jenny's like a reflex and I see something that I have never seen before. It is something about the way she is looking at Johnny, almost quizzical, searching, not listening to Andy's joke at all. I realise that for the first time the outcome of this relationship is not a foregone conclusion and I feel a mixture of hope and nervousness.

* * *

I learnt the full story of Johnny's hybrid background from Jenny later. Born in Malawi to diplomat parents, he spent his early years in East Africa, landing permanently in England for the first time at the age of eleven. Untypically, his parents had resisted the concept of boarding school in the UK, and exposure to a string of local schools that accompanied his parents' moves set him apart from his English peers. He found himself popular yet bored at the same time. He sought stimulation outside the company of humans and found it in time with rocks. His work as a geologist took him initially on extended field trips: weeks spent in the vast, white Altiplano of northern Chile or the tin mines of Bolivia. Promotion had meant that he was now predominantly London-based, though he still made time to visit his parents, now retired in Kenya, and an early girlfriend, now a mother of three and living a few miles from his parents in Naivasha.

I could see why Jenny was attracted to him, beyond the good looks that are a prerequisite in her case. There was a waywardness about him, an edge, a resistance to stereotype, which challenged her. 'What kind of rock would he be if he were a rock?' I asked her once, early on, after that Moroccan dinner.

'I don't know. Jade maybe? I know what you mean, though.'

'What?'

'Well, it's as if something of the rocks that are his life has rubbed off on him.'

'Solid charm and hidden depths – how romantic!'

'Mmm.' And an unfamiliar dreamy look touched her face before she laughed.

Over the weeks that followed I watched something soften in Jenny, as if she were happy for the first time to let her world contract and contain her. In Johnny's company she relaxed into the domesticity of television serials and Indian takeaways, shared walks and shopping lists on a Saturday afternoon. It was the first time that I felt at ease in the company of one of her male partners, without being on my guard or witness to a performance. Two emotions moved within me: a real sense of joy that something was taking her out of herself, out of the blackness which I sensed in her but could do nothing about; and a shiver of jealousy that I could not control.

There were times when the habit of Jenny's personality took over and my own squirming felt all too familiar. On one occasion the three of us were sitting around the kitchen table over an impromptu meal of cheese on toast with red wine when the conversation veered dangerously, led by Jenny.

'Have you ever been unfaithful, Johnny?'

He paused and I thought, *pass the test, please pass the test.*

'Yes, I have, once. I was very young and very naïve and it hurt all of us.'

Oh dear, I thought, *you're slipping – not so intense, not so intense.*

Jenny played her card. 'Well, I hope you don't expect me to be faithful to you. Ownership is not my thing.'

He looked straight at her and then saved himself. He laughed. And laughed. That was Johnny's strength. He challenged her attempts to test him by making fun of her, refusing to be drawn in. Jenny looked momentarily nonplussed by his laughter, and for a glorious split second I thought she was going to let the whole thing go and laugh as well, but then her face hardened into an all too familiar grip.

'So, how young were you? How naïve?' There was something cold and calculated in her tone, which Johnny did not pick up.

'When?' Still laughing.

'When the better half in you rejected the notion of possession by another human being.'

Still totally unaware of the revenge she was about to unleash, he straightened his face into a frown and answered in a mock Cornish accent. 'I were sixteen, me Lord, sixteen and a day.'

'Funny that, isn't it, Pips?'

'What Jenny?' I tried to will calm into her eyes with the coldness of my voice.

'Funny the difference six years makes. Do you think six years would have made a difference to us?'

'Leave it out, Jenny.'

Her eyes anchored Johnny's. 'Pippa and I were abused at the age of ten. You know –raped – if a tongue can rape.'

'For Christ's sake, Jenny, shut up.' I saw a wine glass shatter in slow motion on the table and red wine splash like blood across the unfinished food. I felt Johnny and Jenny staring at me and realised that it was my arm that had thrown the glass. In another slow-motion second I wondered where the brain message that triggered that movement had come from, and then I found myself standing and screaming at Jenny.

'If you want to fuck up the only relationship you've ever had that's worth anything, then do it in private!' And my body left the room, slamming the door behind it. Funny that. It was Jenny who was pushing for a reaction, trying to shock, and me who did in the end.

CHAPTER 47

There are silent tears spilling into the box. So little to show, really. Two diaries, a handful of photos and letters, postcards of her travels, always somehow intimate. There is one from Greece with two old women in black with creased leather faces, laughing into each other's eyes, seemingly unaware of the camera. Perhaps they were.

Pips, you were right, this is one to look after. Johnny is trying to change me and I love it. I feel free and yet with him. The village is gorgeous and our days are spent rambling in mountains and conversation. Next week we chill out on the beach. I am happy and I miss you. Love you always, Jenny.

I feel strange reading these words. A deep sense of irony bites me from within as if I'm facing the sequence of events that came afterwards for the first time. Imagine if flash-forwards to the future existed, how many events would seem unbelievable, laughable even, or just plain intolerable. I imagine life as a pile of bones without the flesh of time to join the different bones together and fatten the relationship between them . . .

They returned, full of themselves and each other. Jenny exuded warmth and laughter, and it occurred to me suddenly that she could be the one to get hurt if things went wrong. Not that there was any reason for things to go wrong. Johnny so obviously cared and she so obviously wanted him to. I began to feel awkward, a superfluous presence between them, and Jenny at last broached the subject of moving out to live with him.

But she never did because something happened first that drew demons like blood from inside her and turned her relationship with Johnny into an impossibility.

When she told me, I responded unthinkingly, with a lump in my throat: 'Oh Jenny, that's fantastic.' And then more slowly, 'My God. Does Johnny –?'

'No, no, he doesn't. Don't tell him, Pips. I don't want him to know. I need to get used to this first, understand how I feel about it, what I'm going to do.'

'But doesn't he need to know? This is about both of you.' There was a vacant look in her eyes, a look of distance that I had not seen for a long time. 'Jenny, aren't you happy about this? It's bound to be a shock, of course you need time to get used to it, but don't cut Johnny out. You should be going through this together.'

'Fuck Johnny! Who said I wanted his baby?'

'Oh Jenny, Jenny, don't do this to yourself. Talk to me, tell me what's going on in your head.'

She looked at me, lost and angry and hurting. 'Don't you see, Pips? Can't you see that it wouldn't work? What if I end up hating him?'

'But why should you?' I knew that something very, very deep-seated in Jenny recoiled from being boxed and defined, and planning the future. I knew the commitment would scare her, but surely not enough to have an abortion?

'Don't you see?' She spoke again between her tears. 'Part of me would love to do this, to be a mother, a wife, to do what other people do, to be normal, but I'm not sure I've got it in me. You . . . you could do it, Pippa, but I don't know if I can.'

'Jenny, if I could do it, so can you. We've got the same scars, the same childhood,' I coaxed her, a huge sense of emptiness rising in me to meet the darkness in her.

She turned on me angrily then. 'It's got nothing to do with being abused. That's all useless fucking history.'

But I persisted. 'It's bound to have affected us in ways that we're still learning about. We never had a father, we were abused by our mother's boyfriend, and our mother accused us of lying, not to mention the fact that she was too busy drinking to be a mother to us most of the time anyway. Don't you think those are scars that might surface when faced unexpectedly with motherhood?'

She looked at me gratefully for a second and gave a tiny, wet laugh. 'Put like that, you may have a point.'

'Jenny, listen,' I pounced on the moment. 'Don't make any quick decisions about this, please, and please talk to Johnny.'

But she refused to tell him, and I watched, helpless, as he struggled to understand her sudden moodiness and her apparent reluctance to follow through with their plans to move into a flat together. I snatched time alone with Jenny to try and work through this thing with her, to help her not to punish herself and Johnny because of something she was not prepared for. I felt sure that it was mostly the shock of it that was getting to her, and the fact that something outside her control was suddenly dictating her life, imposing a responsibility that she had rejected all her life. I knew, too, that Johnny would embrace this die that life had cast and I wished that she would just share this with him and allow them, together, to come to terms with it. I toyed with the idea of telling him, but I knew Jenny would treat that as a betrayal, and I was not prepared to put that between us.

But I did not expect the level of rejection that poisoned her. She spoke of 'it' as if she had swallowed something alien and she blamed Johnny irrationally for deceiving her, for making her think that she could lead a 'normal' life, a life that could be neatly traced in a series of steps leading, in a straight line, to grandchildren and death. She took off for a weekend alone in the Lake District, telling Johnny she needed to think, but not telling him why.

'Pips, I can't go through with it.' She finally cut through any other possibilities. 'I'm going to have an abortion and I don't want Johnny to know. It's over between us. Will you help me?'

'Of course I'll help you, Jenny. You know I'll stand by you whatever you decide, but why does this mean everything is over between you and Johnny?'

'How could I live with him knowing that I had killed his child?'

'It's your child, too, Jenny. The baby is both of yours,' I pleaded.

'No, Pippa, please. It may be mine biologically, but it has nothing to with me mentally or emotionally. I feel as if Johnny has invaded my insides, forced something into me that I do not want, and I know that even if I had this baby, even if I accepted it and came to love it, I would hate its father forever. Johnny deserves more than that.' She looked immeasurably sad.

'Oh Jenny, you're not making sense. Please don't make this decision without talking to Johnny. Why don't you just talk about it together?'

She blinked through wet eyes and her face took on the stoniness that had kept her strong through our childhood. 'If I tell him he'll want to have it. He won't understand how I could possibly not want to. He doesn't have the darkness that's inside me. He'll misunderstand it. He will recoil from me.'

I knew that she was right. Johnny would have seen Jenny with young children, would have marvelled at the lack of self-consciousness and the enthusiasm with which she could slip into the fantasy of their worlds. I had been to her school, seen her working and looking as though she was playing. She never talked down to children, was perpetually curious and reacted to them on their terms, sharing imaginary slug suppers with a three-year old, a rude joke with a fourteen-year-old.

'What makes you so sure that you don't want this baby, Jenny? You love children.' I was running out of words.

'Yes.' She was looking very straight into the mental distance in front of her. 'Yes, I love children and I don't want to bring a child into this world that I cannot be a mother to. I don't have it in me. I just don't have it in me.' She was crying dry, silent tears and I knew there was nothing I could do except be there.

CHAPTER 48

She told Johnny finally, but not until afterwards. At the time, she lied to protect him. Told him three days before her appointment that it could never work between them, that she was not cut out for the commitment of sharing a flat, that she needed space that he could not give her. Her lines were not new, but her suffering on saying them was. Johnny came to me in distress and incomprehension and I colluded in the lie, telling him that this was the way she was, I had seen it before, it was no use trying. He found himself cornered, like Alice, in a world whose dimensions had suddenly changed. He resorted not to resentment, but to pride, and removed himself, more like a neighbour come to borrow sugar at an awkward time than my sister's closest and only real boyfriend.

We came home after the abortion and Jenny let me put her to bed like a baby. The days that followed were sore, quiet days, which blocked out the lengthening light of early summer. Jenny had a sick note, which bought her two weeks to come to terms with what she had done and lost, and I rushed home during lunch breaks to give her food and encouragement as if she were an injured cat. In the hollow of draped rooms she moved like her own shadow and built a new resolution around what she had done.

I came home two days before she was due to return to work to find the curtains drawn, windows wide open and light mopping away the greyness that had gathered inside the flat. Her face was smiling.

'Come on, sis, we're going out. It's over. I am going to drive myself nuts if I carry on like this.'

Over celebratory king prawns and aioli in a tapas bar she told me that she had decided to change everything about her life except her sister. The wheel of fortune had turned in a direction she had not chosen. Well, so be it. She would turn the wheel a little further herself. That way she would gain control again. She loved abandon, but she liked to be in charge of it. I understand so much more about her now.

I told her that Johnny had spoken to me, wanted to see her, wanted to understand what had gone wrong.

'Do you want to stay in touch with him, Pips?'

'Well, of course, I shall miss him, but it's not about that. I just don't think it's fair on either of you to end it like that. This is different to other times. You know it is.'

She paused, counting the cigarette butts in the ashtray between us. 'OK, I'll see him and I'll tell him, but not yet. I can't deal with it yet. I need time to get used to not having him around. Pippa, I'm going to try and find a job outside London. I need to put some distance between this and the rest of my life. You understand, don't you? It's not that I want distance between us, but I think it would do us both good to live separately. It's something we were going to do, after all.'

'Yes, I think you're probably right.' And I did. Most of me did. Probably.

'And another thing. I don't want you to stop seeing Johnny just

SHELAN RODGER

because the relationship between him and me is over. You have become friends, I can see that, and I don't want that to stop just because of me.'

Did she sense something that I didn't?

CHAPTER 49

And so, with the help of changed circumstances – Jenny's new job in a prep school in Sussex, my new flatmate (a quiet, dreamy girl called Karen), a new man in Jenny's life (a painter who lived in Brighton) and a new hobby (bungee jumping) – time slowly put flesh on the bones that otherwise could not have belonged to the same body.

At first I think Johnny hoped that there would be some way back to Jenny through me. He talked incessantly about her, probing for answers that I could not give him, but gradually he talked, imperceptibly, less and less about her, and still we found things to say. There was something protective and solid about him and there were no barriers to get through. We had crossed many bridges in the endless conversations about Jenny, unconsciously revealed and inferred things about each other that were normally taboo, and I ventured opinions in the safety of his company that I would never have offered around a dinner table.

Finally he received a call from Jenny, out of the blue, unforewarned by me, and they met on neutral ground in a pub neither of them knew in central London. I heard about it afterwards from both of them. Johnny said that it was a surprise, but not a shock. He hadn't guessed at the time what it was, but had known she was keeping something from him. To realise that about Jenny meant that he had got a long way – closer than any other man had ever done. He said he felt sad, but that she was right in a way, because it would never have worked in the long term, and yet he hadn't known that then. Jenny was unusually subdued after their meeting. We met at our favourite Café Rouge and I pushed her gently to tell me how it had gone.

'OK, I suppose.'

'Did you tell him everything?'

'I think so. At least I tried to.'

'Oh Jenny, are you OK?' She had that faraway look she sometimes got. It reminded me of me. She nodded slowly, but said nothing. 'Do you have any regrets about it now, Jenny?' I asked as gently as I could. Her reply took a long time to come.

'No,' she said slowly, 'not about what I did, only about who I am.'

* * *

Another summer came and went. Another postcard arrived from Jenny, this one a photo of her taken bungee jumping at Victoria Falls. She returned, high and exuberant, and described the experience to me. She told me it was normal to get bloodshot eyes. The idea of your own blood not being able to keep pace with the speed of your fall was too much for me. Jenny revelled in it.

'You're in this harness thing standing on a bridge to nowhere and when you look down at your feet it's as if you're wearing bifocal lenses. Your feet are in sharp focus and then there is a line where the platform ends across the middle of the lens and everything on the other side is a blur. You switch to long-distance focus and suddenly it seems strange that those feet belong to you. The imminence of what you're about to do takes hold of you in the pit of your stomach. There is no dividing line between physical and mental. Your organs seem to be shouting out from different parts of your body. And then you jump. And you leave a trail of sound behind you, like the vapour trail from a plane. Everybody does, you can't help it, sound floods out of you; some people shout, some people scream, some people laugh.'

I mused in private about doing something like that myself. Not bungee jumping, no way, but going somewhere, like Jenny, on my own. I browsed mentally through some of the remote, glossy landscapes I'd seen in coffee table books and wondered what it would actually be like to stand, alone, at Ayres Rock, or the Grand Canyon, or at the top of one of the world's great waterfalls. I wouldn't need the buzz of the jump to bring the experience alive for me. I would be content to take in the natural wonder on its own terms, as a view to see and breathe and smell. I travelled in my imagination not just to Victoria and Niagara Falls, but to falls my reading took me to: Iguazu Falls on the borders of Argentina, Brazil and Paraguay; the single stream of Angel Falls in the depths of Venezuela's jungle.

Even my new flatmate, dreamy Karen, had been an unlikely participant on a university expedition that had taken her hippo counting in the depths of the Selous Game Reserve in Tanzania. Maybe one day I would surprise people. Maybe one day I would surprise myself.

CHAPTER 50

I did do a trip sooner than I expected, but this one was not alone. Johnny was due to take Sarah, his new girlfriend, to visit his parents in Kenya for Christmas. I had met her only once. Not naturally confident in the kitchen, I had gone to enormous lengths to pre-cook a lamb dopiaza, following each step to the letter in a recipe from one of the *Curry Club Cookbook* series. I took longer than usual to get myself ready, too, uncertain about how to dress, wondering what Sarah would look like. She was beautiful – and blonde. I expected her to be pretty, but for some reason the fact that she was blonde shocked me, as if this were some kind of betrayal to the memory of Jenny. I knew that this was absurd and yet I found myself condemning her for it! She wore a sleek, black dress, in stark contrast to her straight blonde hair, and I regretted my decision to wear jeans.

She and Johnny sat on the sofa and I noticed with a certain relish, which I assumed was associated in some perverse way with a loyalty to my sister, that their body postures did not even remotely mirror each other. Then I realised suddenly that I'd been so intent on my observations that I hadn't noticed the question she'd directed at me.

There was an uncomfortable pause. I felt about ten years old. Johnny broke the silence with laughter. 'Don't worry, you'll get used to Pippa. She spends half her life on another planet!' He said it with warmth, but for the first time something in me rebelled against his ready assumption that he knew me so well. It smacked of an ownership he had no right to. I felt relegated. A momentary look of displeasure flashed on Sarah's face. The familiarity in Johnny's tone of voice had not escaped her, and for a second he was the butt of unspoken anger from two directions.

Then the curry exploded. I had transferred it to a glass dish, which turned out not to be ovenproof. Johnny rushed into the kitchen and, when he realised what had happened, burst out laughing. I forgot where I was and laughed too, till tears wet my eyes. Sarah sat still on the sofa, looking beautiful.

Johnny didn't bother to try and turn us into friends after that, and a certain taboo developed around the subject of Sarah, for reasons that neither of us spoke of. So it came as a surprise when Johnny told me one day, only a month before they were due to go to Kenya, that he had broken it off.

'You didn't like her, did you, Pippa?'

'Well, exploding curries are obviously not conducive to lasting friendships!' I laughed, trying to sidestep what I was honest enough to admit was a totally unfair judgement on my part.

'What was it you didn't like about her?' He pushed me.

'She just seemed so wrong for you, too polished, too shiny.' I couldn't help thinking of rock-related metaphors!

'So, the thing is . . .' He looked uncharacteristically uncomfortable all of a sudden. 'I'm still due to go to Kenya and my parents are expecting me to bring a friend, so why don't you come with me?'

* * *

When I asked Jenny whether she would mind, she took a long time to answer. 'I mean, there's nothing else in it. You do realise that, don't you?' I floundered, wondering what I was doing.

'Pippa, even if there was,' she said finally, very evenly, measuring each word in a way that must have felt alien to her, 'that wouldn't be a reason not to go. If you want to go, go.'

We looked at each other like strangers on a salt plain and I felt for a horrible moment that we were walking backwards, facing each other, but walking away.

CHAPTER 51

The first thing I noticed was the sky. The word that came to my mind again and again when I tried to pinpoint what it was about it that was so different was 'bigger'.

'Don't ever let me attempt to write poetry,' I said to Johnny one languid afternoon after a long curry lunch with his parents. Slightly heady from the wine, we had nevertheless gone for a drive into nearby Hells Gate Park and were sitting on a rocky outcrop, gazing over the plain below.

'And why not?'

Something about the freedom, the spaciousness of this view, fuelled by the wine in my veins, made me want to throw up my arms and burst into song. A gentle recklessness that I was not used to bubbled inside me and I improvised aloud.

Oh the wonder of Kenyan skies
A thousand clouds, a thousand sighs
Bluer and deeper and more alive
Over dry land where acacias thrive.
Compared to the skies we have back home
The skies over here are . . . *bigger*.

'You are the oddest person I've ever met,' said Johnny amidst the laughter that cascaded between us.

His parents were warm, easy people with a gentle disregard for convention, which surprised me. At first his mother struck me as rather prim and proper, but her laugh was like Johnny's, and when it escaped her it was impossible to think of her as a retired diplomat's wife. I watched her reaction one day when their cook broke a glass and cried out in distress with blood streaming from his arm. She washed and dressed the cut, and soothed him with cool, calm words, and I wondered what it would have been like to have had a mother like that. She claimed with a certain pride that Johnny's father had gone bananas since he had retired. At last he could say what he thought to anyone who cared to listen. Years of restrained behaviour and political motives at dinner parties had thrown into relief the things that mattered to him: discussion without an agenda; ideas which did not necessarily lead to action; whisky overlooking the lake; the lazy trust of Colobus monkeys who took their siesta in the trees of their front garden. There was something a little sad, though, in that he had led a life, which, at least at one level, so obviously hadn't suited him, and it made me look inwards and wonder what was really important to me. What did I want out of life?

Johnny took me on safari. We drove to a patch of coast south of Mombasa and then back through Tsavo National Park. We were away for ten days. We were sitting in complete and comfortable silence on the stone veranda of one of Ngulia's bandas, overlooking what was surely one of the most peacefully green valleys in the world, when it happened, finally. It was early evening, just before dusk, and the grey, slow-motion shapes of elephants swayed close to the river below us. I was transfixed, and it took time for it to filter into my consciousness that I, too, was being watched. Where do we get that sixth sense from? The certainty that someone is looking at us or following us? My skin prickled with sudden self-consciousness and I felt the blood colouring my face, delaying the moment when I would need to turn and face his eyes. 'Pippa, come here,' was all he said.

I wish I could say that we made love like moonstruck lovers who melt into each other's bodies and find their souls. Or first-time lovers, who discover each other with slow, deliberate exploration as if they are remembering the other person's body to paint it later. Or old lovers, so familiar with each other's habits and desires that their shared orgasm is as sure and safe as the strokes which lead to it. Or uninhibited lovers, whose screams follow whispered fantasies of another woman's breasts.

But our lovemaking was not like any of that. We did not make love like lovers. We made love like friends, with a bashful warmth, a gentle fervour, which was somehow sexless and failed to banish the taboos that lurked beneath the surface. The transgression of friendship. The long sexual silence in my life since Eddie. Jenny.

When he came finally, quietly, almost apologetically, I turned away from him and cried, quietly, apologetically. He held me and, in sleep, we became lovers at last, wrapped in the smell of each other's skin.

CHAPTER 52

'Pippa, it's OK, I don't mind. I have no right to mind, but I don't mind. I don't want you to feel bad.'

Two emotions welled inside me: gratitude and irritation. These were emotions that didn't, shouldn't, go together. She had spoken immediately, not even waiting to find out what had happened, whether there was any need to say what she had decided to say. That was so typical of Jenny. She was so sure of herself and, of course, she was right. She had tapped straight into the guilt she sensed in me the moment we saw each other again. I felt tongue-tied, as I so often had as a child, relying on Jenny to say what I was thinking, to tell me what I was thinking, yet I knew this was unfair. I knew that she was being generous and I knew that this was exactly what I needed to hear. I needed to know that it wouldn't come between us.

'It won't come between us, you know.'

'You cow!' I laughed at last. 'Do you remember Mrs Forster?'

'Yes?'

'I remember the first time I went to her house and she kept embarrassing me by saying what I was thinking. Am I so transparent that my thoughts are written all over my face? Am I really so mind-bogglingly dull? Is there no mystery behind this forehead?'

'You're delirious!'

'I'm happy. Thank you, Jens.'

We laughed and hugged and got drunk.

We never spoke about what had actually happened in Kenya. In time it became quite natural to speak about my relationship with Johnny. In time their shared past became a story in a photo album with no claims on the present. The only subject where references were oblique was our sex life. It was the only thing that was ever taboo between us. Maybe Jenny had learnt after all that, in some cases, 'not telling' is better for everyone.

Dreamy Karen got married and Johnny moved in with me. Slowly we had learnt to create the distance from friendship we needed to allow us to discover each other again, as lovers. Slowly we moved beyond the highs of discovery into the mixed landscape of the stable couple, where gentle power games creep in and hitherto unimportant facets of domestic life become the battleground for asserting control. Shoes, which appear to have walked willy-nilly all over the flat, a teaspoon left in the wrong place, music at the wrong volume – the clash of insignificant habits becomes a reason to doubt compatibility, yet in this landscape there were many moments of comfortable camaraderie and affection, flashes of insight, pleasure shared.

And then everything changed.

CHAPTER 53

Unlike Jenny, I was never qualified to teach. I drew on my knowledge of learning another language and my imagination. I delved into my own love of Spanish and came to the conclusion that speaking another language allows you to recreate yourself, without the inhibitions you assume, wrongly, are an innate part of your character. I was shocked and delighted to discover that one of my very first students, who spoke English with remarkable fluency, had a stammer in his own language. English held none of the associations that stifled his confidence in Spanish, and speaking a foreign language allowed him to redefine himself.

I sought students whose level of English was already good enough to act as a doorway and I helped them through to the possibilities that lay behind it. I assumed that people were fundamentally creative and that even the sternest bank managers loved fantasy. The teacher's mask gave protection. The intimacy of one-to-one gave freedom.

There is a lesson I love. Conditional tenses: *if X hadn't happened, I wouldn't have done Y. If I hadn't done Y, I wouldn't be here . . .*

I ask you to make a list of all the things in your life you feel good about, anything at all: a relationship, a hobby, where you live, an aspect of your job. Then I ask which is the most tenuous, the most 'surprising', and we string together a whole list of coincidences that have led to the present. We glorify the past; we turn it into a story.

Then I take you one step further. I ask you to imagine where you would like to be in five years' time. Who do you want to be with? What do you want to be doing? Now I ask you to jump into this ideal future and explain how you got there. And again we create a story, but this one is even more powerful. This one taps something inside you that the day to day buries. This one dresses your secret desires in the safety of conditionals and you leave the lesson with a strange feeling of optimism. That is my strength.

But there is also a downside. Alone, it is easier to be drawn to regret; there is a darkness in turning life into a string of conditionals. It is a darkness I have learnt to live with.

If Jenny had not got pregnant, she might have stayed with Johnny. They might have worked things out. If she had not pushed him away, he would not have turned to me for understanding, grown so close to me. If I hadn't accepted his invitation to Kenya, he would probably have met someone else, someone more suitable, someone who had nothing to do with Jenny or me. If Johnny and I had not started a relationship, Jenny and I would have spent more time together than we did. Maybe I could have helped her. Perhaps she would have settled. But she didn't.

Her bungee jumping became a symbol, a clue to her obsession with escape. If I hadn't inspired her with second-hand pictures of Angel Falls and Iguazu, perhaps she wouldn't have decided to go to South America. If she'd chosen another trip, if she'd chosen to do a camel safari in Africa or Australia, to climb a mountain in India or tour the jazz clubs of

America, she wouldn't have been on the Austral flight. She would not have died.

And if she had not died, something in me would not have died. If I had not lost so much, I would not have been driven to find her. I wouldn't have followed in her footsteps. I wouldn't have walked out on Johnny without explanation, much as she did, and turned my life upside down by coming to Argentina, where it happened.

If I hadn't felt somehow guilty, I wouldn't have blamed myself for not being there for her. If I hadn't wanted so very badly to understand her, to be near her, I wouldn't have needed her identity to cloak my loneliness. I wouldn't have sought to discover what it was that I had failed to understand about her. I wouldn't have tried to reach her by bringing her ghost to life.

But her absence tore me apart. I, Pippa, did not exist, could not exist without Jenny. When I checked into the hotel on the day I arrived in Buenos Aires and they asked me my name, I heard myself say, in a voice that was no longer mine, 'Jenny.' My name is Jenny. Pippa is gone.

PART THREE

CHAPTER 54

My days have a pattern. I have lined them with the soft cushions of routine. I wake early, momentarily thrown by the sunlight funnelling through my small bedroom window and a snatched glimpse of the sea. I walk across the dirt divide between my lodgings and the taverna where I work, past a dog still sleeping and the distant sound of a cock crowing beyond the point where the villas end. Breakfast is the same every morning: fruit and honey, creamy yoghurt and thick, black coffee. I eat alone, grateful, and staring into nowhere.

Mornings are my own. I fill them with chores and the sea. The beach here is made of a kind of shingle, which turns silver underwater. I swim in endless green and feel, not peace, but a calmness that all the routine in the world cannot give me on land. My skin is nutmeg brown in the water. Later I will spend hours on my feet, going back and forth between kitchen and verandah, taking orders, carrying trays heaped with Greek salad, calamari and cold beer for the tourists. They will be both disappointed and relieved to discover that I speak English and will ask me to explain bits of the menu to them, assuming that I speak Greek. They will not know that I have learnt just the bare minimum, that the curiosity which used to make me good at languages is paralysed somewhere inside me. Some will ask me how long I've been here, what I'm doing here, and I will feed them reluctant snippets with none of the fervour that flavoured my CV in Buenos Aires.

The restaurant owners, a couple in their sixties, are delighted to have an English girl on their staff and treat me with a gently paternalistic benevolence. The father says I have my head in the clouds, but I am a good worker. He catches me sometimes, silently watching the couples on holiday. I have stopped reading books, but I still invent other people's lives.

I sleep briefly in the space of the afternoon between the last round of lunch dishes and the first round of evening preparations. In the soft early evening light, as tourists are having their showers, Greek men draw up their seats to play cards, while their women huddle together to talk about them and make food for them. The setting sun draws the tourists to our restaurant. It is further to walk from the centre of the town, but our verandah has a view straight across the water into the sunset. The light turns even burnt bald patches golden. Then, as if suddenly remembering where it needs to be, blinks and is gone. Now the couples turn their attention to each other and more alcohol. By the time the evening is over, my body aches and the exhaustion is a pillow, which gently smothers any possibility of thought.

The only day I find it difficult to sleep is my free day. My body is grateful for the rest, but my mind becomes active in spite of all my attempts to lull it into thinking that this is simply a variation on a theme, a day like any other. I take my moped and splutter into the hills inland. I explore the beaches and pretend to be a tourist, trying in vain to read, or I succumb to well-meant invitations to join local fishing trips. Yet my mind digs a hole in these days and the hole is a cave into the past.

CHAPTER 55

There was a certain symmetry about my departure from Argentina, which Nick would have found comic. I had arrived, vomiting, and changed my name. After a year-long pilgrimage, culminating in a thwarted attempt to reunite with my dead sister at the edge of a waterfall, I had turned away and got on a plane again. I had vomited in the airplane toilets, wondering what possible kick the mile-high club get out of the exchange of bodily fluids in a venue so cramped and smelly, and I had recognised the old Pippa again.

The vomiting was, I assumed, a perfectly unimaginative attempt by my body to flush out what my mind could not deal with. I told the curious, pony-tailed, Spanish air traffic controller who happened to be in the seat next to me that I was pregnant and maybe, unbeknown to my conscious self, that was a metaphor for something hopeful in this new departure.

There was a drawer that I battled to keep closed. Ignacio. I tried to be like Jenny, I tried to own the decision and not blame life, but it hurt, and I was shocked by how much more it hurt than what I did to Johnny when Jenny died. I ached all over and I longed for Ignacio's touch to massage the pain away.

I was still angry with Jenny. It was as if she had disappeared in the middle of a play and I was left, facing the audience, ad-libbing madly and glancing surreptitiously backstage to see where she was hiding. I imagined the glint of mischief on her face. It had been there all the way through our childhood in games that went too far for Pippa, but never far enough for Jenny.

It wasn't until the Spanish controller was slumped in sleep and we were halfway across the world that I asked Pippa what the fuck she was going to do. I had changed. There were old doors I knew I could no longer open. Johnny, Brixton bookshops, dreamy Karen, Jenny's address book – these had to remain figments of memory. I felt as if I had been given witness protection, a new identity that meant I couldn't go back to the same places and people that were part of my past, yet the house and the instructions that should be part of the new programme were missing.

I had enough cash for about two nights in a dodgy B&B. I went north of the river just in case, and then chance told me what to do. On my second day back in London, having just discovered that I had an English bank balance of £69.69 (Jenny would have loved that!) I wandered into an internet café with the intention of seeing what my money could buy. I found:

- A special offer on a pair of DKNY sunglasses
- A week's car hire with Hertz in Spain
- A leather-bound Filofax with a list of famous people's birthdays and a picture of Princess Di
- A case of Pinot Grigio
- A subscription for some obscure book society

- A red lipstick (I had no idea it was possible to spend so much on a lipstick!)
- A ticket to a town I had never heard of on mainland Greece

The flight was the following day. The ticket cost £69.00, so I left 69 pence in my bank account as an investment in my future and got on another plane.

CHAPTER 56

I honestly don't think I made the connection at first. I was so intent on the need to secure, fast, at the very least, board and lodging and, with a bit of luck, some pocket money, that I didn't stop to question, or to feel insecure, or shy, or absolutely anything. I simply acted. This was fresh, novel, almost enjoyable. At the airport I spotted a tour bus. Perfect. Where the tourists went is where there would be work, so while the tour guide fussed on a mobile phone I managed to hide myself in the mess of people trailing onto the bus. I sat at the back and listened as Janet gave us tips about the natives and how to fit into the local community, including the fact that the sun was very hot and we should always wear sun cream. I found my taverna, and my family with a spare room and the will to take me on, and then it dawned on me that, of all the places I could have chosen, I had come to my father's home country.

Now it nags at me, that knowledge, and lies in wait in the underground of the days when thought has space to find me, and I realise that I am going to try to find him, but I need the routine of these sun-washed days to settle me first. Is this just another fiction?

Is this the sensible side of the reef? Jenny, what do you think? You were always determined you never wanted to find him. What comfort could there be in a reunion with a man capable of leaving the mother of his children before they were born? But I want to know why. I want to know what he looks like. I want details about him that will fill in the gaps where my imagination fails.

We found wedding photos once, at the back of a writing desk, and Jenny sneaked them up to the attic, so that we might pore over them in open, honest curiosity, without the shadow of Mother's disapproval, but they were hand-ripped to cut him out, and tell-tale smudges of spilt tears and vodka blurred our mother's smile. I wonder where she is now. Does she even know about her daughter's death?

How important is blood anyway? Why is it that a perfectly normal, contented and well-loved adoptee can feel driven to find their real mother? Is it just the lure of the 'what if?', latent in all of us, perhaps more powerful in someone who knows they are adopted? Is it just a yearning for our roots? The drive to understand the history or culture that has gone into the bloodline that has produced us?

I have no answers, only questions. Perhaps that is a good sign. Perhaps curiosity is coming back. Perhaps new answers can fill in the gaps. I really am going to try and find him, Jenny. I have his name, I can guess his age, I will use the net. I have decided.

CHAPTER 57

I make a note of the date – 15 August 1998 – at the back of my address book. There is already a short list of dates, which reads like a topsy-turvy birthday list with no names, or an attempt to encode the pin numbers that will be forgotten by the time you get back from holiday. There is no code, however. They are quite simply dates that are important in my life. The day Jenny and I said goodbye at a train station on our paths from childhood to different cities; the day I lost my virginity (willingly); the day of Jenny's abortion, the Friday that will stay with me forever; the day that I was tempted to jump at Iguazu Falls (yes, Ignacio was right to be nervous). Usually these dates are committed to paper retrospectively, but whatever the outcome of today, there is enough history behind it for me to know in advance that this day belongs to the list of key dates in my life.

In the process of finding my father I found an uncle, my father's brother, who passed on the coded question that I knew only the man who really was my father would be able to answer. I asked, 'What did you find in the bosom of the woman you married?' She had an uncommonly prominent mole, perched like a third nipple between her breasts.

And now, today, I am in Athens and we have agreed to meet in a café in a square. I have told him I will be wearing a blue dress. It is a deep dark blue and I have contact lenses behind my sunglasses. I am early so that I can be the one to see him arrive, but I suspect that he may have done the same, and so I look around me nervously as I find a seat with the view that I need. Jenny, wouldn't you like to be here with me now? Admit it, just once! But Jenny is quiet.

A bulbous, dark man of around sixty is crossing the square and loping towards me. His eyes dart from side to side, taking in the shape of a woman's bottom whenever one passes, while his big body struggles. No, no, oh please don't let it be him. I catch a glimpse of his stomach, hairy and protruding through buttons that are tired of holding him in. He has not seen me and I think I have time still. I could just get up and walk away. I don't want to be this man's daughter. OK, Jenny, you were right again. Oh no, he is still coming towards me. An image of the Blue Masturbating Machine dances somewhere inside my eyelids and Frank laughs in the shadows.

In my haste to get away I do two things. I knock over a glass, which smashes onto the floor, drawing eyes from everywhere, and I collide with a man who is thin, like celery.

'Sorry, I am so sorry,' I say, stepping backwards, wanting to cry, but he grips my arm and I hear my name.

'Pippa?' Impossibly, he says my name.

And I see him for the first time. The lines in his face are deep and comfortable, lines that look as though they have grown from living and laughing, rather than emerging indiscriminately through the passage of time. The eyes are dark and bright and have none of the soft blur so often a product of ripening age. This, then, is my father. Thank God.

His English is clipped and hesitant at first, but as we talk the deep furrows on his warm face relax and his sentences grow longer and smoother, like snakes waking up in the sun. I ask him question after question, deflecting the focus from me and genuinely hungry for the details of his life.

'You are very intense,' he laughs softly. 'Very different to your mother.'

'What was she like when you met her?' I hadn't wanted to discuss her. It was us I wanted to talk about and yet I cannot stifle the urge to discover something new about her, something innocent, something I could use to dim my resentment against her. My father looks at me for a long time, as if he is being asked to complete an impossibly long mathematical calculation or as if he is weighing something very heavy in his mind. Perhaps he can no longer remember the words in English for what he wants to say.

'She was full of bubbles,' he says finally, with affection, 'like a – how do you say in English – a brook, like a brook, or champagne.'

That's more like it, I think, but when I look at my father I see there is no irony there, only nostalgia. Why did he leave her, I wonder? There is something not right. This is not the evil, heartless villain of our mother's sob story, but then maybe time has changed him. Time, which coats torturers and dictators in gentle layers of humanity, so that by the time they are grandfathers they have become merely old men, no better or worse than any other.

'Now you,' he says, sitting back and looking straight at me. 'I am tired of talking. Let me hear you talk.'

Normally this is the kind of line that freezes me, that fills me with fear on a first date. It was easier being Jenny. I learnt from her. I learnt how to warm up to this kind of line, how to deliver lies upon lies, unflinching, through the comfort of contact lenses, but this time there is none of that. Now I am relaxed.

I am sitting at a café in Athens with my father and there is a deep and immediate recognition between us. I tell him about Jenny and about Argentina. I don't mention that I lived in her name. I think that's too much to tell the father you meet for the first time in your life, but I feel I might be able to tell him one day and that knowledge is like hot milk inside me, warming me from within.

We talk into the evening and we go for dinner. I learn that I have two half- brothers, teenagers, two years apart in time and ten years apart in taste and character. My mind is beginning to race with the wine and I can feel it fast-forwarding through my future, catching indeterminate glimpses of myself in the heart of this new family. Slow down, slow down, I think to myself, switching wine for water. No more wine tonight. There is too much emotion and I want to stay in the present. Neither of us wants to speak about what actually happened. We are in a tango dance together, avoiding the unmentionable with our heads held high.

When I go to bed it is 16 August and it occurs to me that all the dates I have recorded in my address book are to do with loss. All but this one.

CHAPTER 58

You see, Jenny, it was worth it. I have taken the biggest emotional risk in my life and it has paid off. We have a father. He is a good man. You can see it in his eyes. I always was better at reading people's eyes, wasn't I? I knew Frank's eyes were bad, right from the first day he walked into our house, but our father's eyes are bright. Nothing lurks there waiting to come out. I don't know what went wrong or why he left us. One day he will tell me. One day I will ask him, but there is no hurry. We have arranged to meet again in a couple of weeks. He is going to come and visit me here.

Andreas, the owner of the taverna, will not stop teasing me. He has seen me smiling. He is convinced I have found a boyfriend and I haven't the heart to tell him I have found a father. His family works together, plays together, grows together like grapes on a vine. What would he make of my story? No, I haven't the heart and yet I need to think up some kind of explanation for my father's visit.

It's because I am distracted in such thoughts that I don't notice anything significant about the latest sun-drenched, blonde-haired tourists who wander in to choose their table and gaze across the water.

They come and go, these postcard couples. Under the spell of sea and sunshine and sex every night, with no football to compete for his attentions, they fall in love again and again. There is no apple of temptation here, no mates or habits that she cannot stand, no credit card-statements, no demands on him to notice when she is wearing something new. They are naked together in the safety of the knowledge, unspoken, that this is time-bound. Leave them here for six months and the apples will grow, for all the sea and sunshine in the world cannot stop the apples.

I have developed the ability to take an order on the outside and on the inside compose songs or paintings, my own private odes to the lives of the many who pass before me. It is when I hear the word 'bollocks' said in a tone of rollicking dismissiveness I recognise instantly that the inside and the outside collide.

'Bollocks, it's political correctness gone mad. Policeperson, spokesperson, person this, person that . . . I'm not "manning" the shop guv, honest, I'm "personing" the shop. What a load of crap!'

'Nick, how are you?' I place two menus on the table. 'Fucking hell . . . Jenny! What on earth are you doing here?'

There follows a flurry of hugs and incredulous laughter, while one piece of the back of my mind wonders how to tell him that my name is Pippa and another piece of my mind wonders if we will still get on, if I haven't changed too much for us to be friends.

'You're different!' he says, and steps back to look me up and down.

'I've changed my name,' I blurt with false confidence, as if it is the most natural thing in the world, like a new haircut.

'You fucking maniac!' he laughs. He is really pleased to see me. His girlfriend looks uncomfortable.

'Are you going to introduce us?' she intervenes.

'Sorry, Mel, this is a really good friend of mine. We met in Argentina. Her name is . . .'

'Pippa,' I interject.

'Pippa!' Nick can't help himself. 'What the fuck kind of name is that? Of all the names you could have chosen, you chose Pippa. Why Pippa, for God's sake?'

Mel is looking at me with blatant mistrust. It's alright, honestly, I want to reassure her. I am not some secret psychopath, sprung from nowhere to taunt you.

'It chose me,' I say. This does nothing to change me in the eyes of Mel. Nick is almost choking on his own laughter.

'Ever the woman of mystery!'

Yeah, I think, the one tin can you couldn't open, but I think this with pleasure, not malice.

'Bring us a drink then, so that we can raise a glass to you, woman. I thought you'd fallen off the face of the planet. It's good to see you!'

CHAPTER 59

'Tell a woman you love her often enough and she won't notice that you don't. Mr Kipling bakes exceedingly good cakes. It doesn't matter if you think they taste like shit or you once met someone who worked in a Mr Kipling cake factory and told you the same cakes went into Sainsbury's boxes. We want to believe what people tell us. We're all gluttons for repetition. Look at politics, for God's sake. We vote for our politicians not because of what they do, but because of what they say. And it's not just private companies that are cashing in, it's the public services. You remember, the "sacred" ones, the ones that made us proud to be British when we lived in the Third World. "Lambeth National Health – putting people first . . ." As opposed to what, for fuck's sake? Stethoscope maintenance? Nurses' pay? No matter, it makes me feel good when I go to a doctor in Lambeth. I know that if there are any dogs in the queue, they will see me first. It's me that counts!'

'You're not starting to develop a social conscience, are you Nick?' I ask him, laughing over the brandies between us. This is classic Nick drunken drivel. Nothing is safe from the knife edge of his cynicism and yet there is something clean about it. He says what he thinks. He doesn't care what other people think, a bit like Jenny, except Jenny was always pushing for reactions. In a way I envy both of them.

'Take the company I was telling you about,' he gabbles on, ignoring my comment, 'the one that wanted advice on their branding strategy. Do you know the difference between organic growth and growth through acquisition?'

'Fuck off, Nick, I haven't been away that long.'

'Just checking. Well, they had acquired about a dozen different organisations. Their branding was all over the place, an alphabet soup of different logos and standards, but basically they had it sussed, because they paid enough lip service to the idea that it was people that mattered. So their employees worked their buns off and looked the other way when those who were surplus to requirements in the newly acquired organisations were made redundant.'

'What's your point, Nick?'

'The point is that they took things at face value, because what was being said was what they wanted to hear.'

I have a momentary flashback, a vision of my mother, quietly wringing her hands and saying, 'It didn't happen.'

How on earth did Nick land a job in consultancy? He says it was someone he knew who got him the job, someone who 'owed him one', someone who just happened to work in a company that offered 'branding solutions'. I couldn't imagine how he had ever got through the first interview, but he had become their best researcher, the one they sent out to get under the skin of how people felt about the company they worked for or did business with, what the company stood for in their eyes. Opening tin cans – yes, it made sense that Nick should find his niche in a line of work that delved into human motivation and then served it up with a new logo.

I look at Nick with blurred vision and notice that he is smirking. His head cocked to one side, his eyes, bloodshot and marble blue, taking me in, and a sudden distance springs up between us. I think of his girlfriend, asleep, alone on the last night of their one-week holiday, and I feel guilty. I didn't want to take away your last Greek orgasm, I want to say to her, it's just that we haven't seen each other since he left Argentina. There is so much to catch up on and only one night to do it before he returns – with you – to England. He is fond of you, you know. He told me so after you left us. Will it last? I don't know. He is unsure, I think, underneath it all, of who he wants to be, but aren't we all? Would Ignacio and I have lasted if I hadn't run away? But the woman Ignacio was drawn to wasn't really me . . . and my reasoning buries the question.

'Jenny?' Nick's hand has brushed my face to bring me round.

'Pippa,' I say.

There is a space, which could turn into laughter, or curiosity, or concern. In the end I get confusion.

'I don't think I can call you Pippa, Jenny.'

It's late. We've both had too much to drink. We both miss the humour of his words. It occurs to me suddenly that Jenny, the real Jenny, would have been the perfect woman for him. I feel something flush through me, something between sadness and irritation. Bollocks, I think, looking at Nick with affection. I am overemotional. Nick has dealt well with the drama I have offered up to him tonight. Between the teasing and the revelling he has accepted the story that fell from me finally in simple sentences to shut him up. He has done something for me tonight that no one else could. He has understood.

'Nick,' I say, reaching over to ruffle his hair. 'If we're going to stay in touch, you're going to have to start calling me Pippa.'

'What about Pips?'

'Definitely not.'

'Or old slag?'

I shake my head, laughing.

'Nutter?'

'Nope.'

'Gorgeous?'

'Go to bed.'

'Pippa, then – on one condition.'

'What's that?'

'You call me Hunk.'

CHAPTER 60

There is a slackness in me after Nick has gone. It's as if I've been breathing in for weeks, and the act of letting go for just one night has destroyed the muscle tone in my stomach. I feel as if I need to wear a wet suit to hold me in again. I swim further out to sea than I have ever dared.

And I take another emotional risk, more of a ritual perhaps than anything else, like throwing a pebble into the sea: I send a postcard to the last known address I have for my mother. The words find their way, somehow, from the act of finding my father.

Dear Mother,

I don't know if this will reach you, but I want you to know that I have found our father. I don't understand, Mother. He seems a good man. What happened? What on earth went wrong? I am sorry, this is not very fair after so long, but there are pieces of my life that I need to recover after what happened . . .

Does she even know about Jenny's death, I wonder in a moment of ice, or will she think I'm talking about Frank? I let the ambiguity lie.

I hope you are OK.

I am grateful for the boundaries of the postcard. I hesitate, and a lame tide wells up inside me.

If you want to contact me, here is my email address . . .

I get a message from my father saying that he cannot make it on the date we had planned, but suggesting we meet in Athens again, a week later. Light with relief that I will not have to deal in either lies or truth to explain my father's presence here, I ask Andreas if I can change my day off. His wife nods knowingly at him and he touches my arm gently, as if he were my own father giving his blessing to a first date.

* * *

I wake up one morning light-headed with the remnants of a dream. I have to fight the sense of certainty that I have been talking to Jenny. I was falling through clouds when I saw her. She seemed to be sunbathing on the wing of a plane, suspended in midair, a look of serenity on her face that I had never seen before.

'Jenny, what are you doing here?' I ask her, budging her along with my shoulder as I settle beside her, legs dangling over the silver edge to nowhere.

'This is where I live,' she laughs. 'It's not that bad, really – fantastic view and I bump into all-sorts up here. You'd be surprised.'

'What do you mean, Jenny?' She taps me and points at a puffy yellow cloud, a few feet away from us.

'Isn't he gorgeous?'

She has her own Greek god living on a cloud next door. I laugh and hug her.

'It's good to see you, Jens. I thought you'd deserted me.'

'Never,' she says, and I feel whole again.

I realise that there are voices all around us and I begin to see people coupled with all manner of objects, swarming through my vision.

'Why does everyone seem attached to something?' I ask, confused.

'It's our version of an address: the circumstance of our deaths, the anchor to our previous lives. Mine is the wing of a plane. There are others on staircases, in cars, rivers, mountain crevices. There is one old goat who died from a stroke in the middle of an orgasm with a prostitute. He will spend the rest of his after-life sleeping with her! We're the lucky ones. The others are in hospital beds surrounded by tubes and machines.'

'But it sounds horrible, Jenny,' I say, unable to believe that she can stay so calm.

'Oh no, it's not that bad. There's no pain, you see, and these are only our addresses, the place where we sleep. We can come and go as we please during the day. We can choose the age we want to be for the day, or at least any age we were before we died. There are babies here who will never grow up and old people who choose to play with them one day and mother them the next. You can't get bored, because there's so much variation, so much unpredictability. I tell you what,' she says, leaning towards me, with a look of mischief that is so familiar I feel like crying. 'It makes for some very interesting perspectives on sex.'

'You're allowed to have sex?' I say, incredulous.

'Of course we are. What kind of an afterlife would it be with no sex? You see Tom over there, the one I showed you on the yellow cloud? He died in a parachute jump when he was twenty-seven.

Anyway, I've had sex with him on the day before he died, when he was excited about the jump he was going to do for charity, and then I changed his nappy the following day!'

'So you're OK, then?' I laugh, not altogether comfortable with the concept she has just offered me, but focusing on what I need to know to take back with me.

'Yes, I'm fine. I miss you, but I'm not going anywhere, and one day we'll be together again.'

A bus is drawing towards us across a roll of cloud and I realise with the conviction of dreams that it is my bus. Time to go.

'Thanks, Jens. See you soon.'

'OK, Tootlepips. See you Sunday.'

A piece of ice shoots through me. 'What did you say, Jenny?'

'See you some day.'

'Oh yeah, OK, see you some day. I love you.'

I feel cold and warm all day after this dream. I am an atheist. I do not believe in spirits, although I think that perhaps people's energy stays with us in ways that we do not understand. The dream is so obviously a kind of wish fulfilment, giving me the reassurance I crave that Jenny is fine, that we will see each other again, and yet I find the details disturbing. I am scared by what my mind is capable of inventing – and of how real Jenny seemed. No matter how hard I fight it, I feel as if something has happened, as if some kind of communication has taken place.

I wonder what Ignacio would make of this, and I want to reach out suddenly to Ana, ask her all the questions I shied away from in Buenos Aires. Does your sister visit you in your sleep? How do you live without her? How does someone whose sister has been tortured ever smile again?

CHAPTER 61

I have started a relationship. I marvel at it. A truly postmodern relationship, carefree yet risk-free, constantly redefining itself, spinning out of control and yet utterly under control, fantastically penetrative without invasion or possession, and it doesn't matter what I look like when we meet. I could have acne and be dressed in a sack and he would still find me exciting. It's true love, fuelled by that greatest stimulant of all – the imagination!

We met only a week ago and already he has seen more sides of me than most men would see in a lifetime. He is changeable, unpredictable, challenging, exciting. He has let me into his deepest fantasies and I am happy to be the cliché – his housewife in the kitchen, his whore in the bedroom.

I am happy because he fulfils a need that lies somewhere deep in many women and because there is no threat. I can come in the safety of knowing that, even though we have only known each other for a matter of days, there is absolutely no danger of contracting anything from him. It used to alarm me that Jenny could be so unafraid and unaware of the risks of unprotected sex. She always assured me she used a condom, but I didn't believe her.

We met in a chat room for the nearly thirties. None of that what shall I wear, do I look OK, what will he think of me crap. It was love at first word! There is something peculiarly powerful about the opportunity a virtual affair can give you. It's hard to make mistakes, or to judge or be judged. It is a constant process of discovery and invention, a game where the rules can change whenever you want them to.

At least that is how I feel for the first few days. I have opened a door deep inside and I let our fantasies mingle and meet and spark off each other. I give vent to the sexual frustration that doubtless has been building inside me, despite me, in the months that have gone by. Do I wonder who the person is behind the words? No. There is no person behind the words, just concepts. The mystery is a source of excitement in itself, a source of opportunity, just as darkness can sometimes be more of a stimulant than making love with the light on. I feel closer to Jenny, more authentically close than I felt when I tried to live out her lifestyle in Buenos Aires, trying to have sex for the sake of it. It is as if I am learning about sex all over again, as Pippa this time, gaining my own insight into the pleasure that silver-lined so much of Jenny's darkness.

And then one single thought is enough to bring the whole venture crashing down on me. I wake with a start one night: how do I know that it isn't Frank, the man who abused us, the man who deceived our mother, the paedophile. Frank's eyes are there, gloating in the darkness. A can of worms has spilled itself into my brain. It could be anyone. Frank or the Blue Masturbating Machine, a man with a wife and children asleep in the next room or a man too old to get an erection, a man who has raped his sister or a pimply underage adolescent. I feel sick, physically sick with something I will never get rid of. I push it down, this can of worms, down into the deepest part of me, down into a part of me that only Jenny will ever come near.

CHAPTER 62

My father seemed preoccupied the last time I saw him. I think he shares my preference for the anonymity of a bar or restaurant in Athens to anything more personal.

'So, tell me about Buenos Aires. What was it like?' A safe question, and I rose to it.

'Well, when I first saw it from the sky, I nearly panicked. It just looked like this ghastly flat endless concrete smear on the earth.'

'Smear?' He always asks me to explain a word he doesn't know.

'Like a stain, when you drop red wine on the carpet.'

'Ah, I see . . .' I waited for the signal to go on and it came eventually, but the pause was a long one.

'Anyway,' I continued, 'when you are down at street level, the trees make it bearable. I loved the sense of street life they have. When one of the top teams wins an important football match, people of all ages just pour onto the street, beating saucepans and drums. There is always noise. Sometimes it's suffocating, but there is something vibrant about it.'

'Vi– vibrant. I think I know that word. Yes . . .' Again that long pause, when it's hard to tell if he is thinking of the right words in English or just thinking. 'Yes, your mother was vibrant and you, you too are vibrant, like your mother.'

I wasn't used to being called vibrant and I wasn't used to being compared to my mother. I found it disconcerting and he sensed it, seamlessly changing the subject. 'But tell me more about Buenos Aires.'

And so goes our tango dance. Measured swerves and arcs, painlessly sidestepping any hint of danger or mediocrity that might threaten the ease between us. I do not know enough about Greek men to know what is typical about him, but I sense a deep-seated lack of convention by any culture's standards. He combines a childlike curiosity with a sensitivity that leaves the object of his curiosity intact. Whether the object is a book, a person or a political view, his approach is the same. He is like a lion that pads around his prey, observing not to kill, but to learn and to protect. Maybe this is called tolerance. What do you think, Jenny? Is that what he is, what he stands for? Tolerance? So why did he walk out on Mother? Every now and again, as we dance across Athens, the question wakes up and gnaws at my ankles like a homeless rat.

I sense his reluctance to introduce me to his real life and family, and I am sensitive to this. Was this what was on his mind last time? Did he think I would hold it against him? I tried to reassure him by showing that I was happy just to be in his company, without defining what this meant, leaving our tango to run its course.

We stood at the top of the Acropolis, overlooking the dwindling hordes of camera-noosed tourists. The month of September, too, was waning and my father, gently circling, asked me a question.

'Pippa, your work is going to stop. What will you do?'

I didn't know. 'I think I will go back to England. I think I need to find a job to go back to.' This was a very simple thing to say, and as I said it I believed in it. I had done enough ghost-hunting.

'Do you want to go back?' The lion padded closer, but I felt no fear.

'I think I do.' This was what it was like to be defenceless and safe at the same time. I had not felt anything like it since Jenny left me, but then suddenly, perversely, I felt extremely lonely. My father sensed it. He held me in his thin arms and we just stood there, saying nothing. We walked then, father and daughter, side by side. For all Mother's comments about our olive looks, I could see no physical resemblance between my father and me, or Jenny.

'Do I look anything like your sons?' I wondered abruptly.

My father frowned, just as abruptly. Was this too much then, too inquisitive?

'I didn't mean . . .' I faltered, wanting to reach for my glasses. When I'm nervous I still forget I've got contact lenses, I still miss the physical sensation of something between me and the rest of the world.

'No, no,' he interrupted. 'You are OK to ask. It is just . . .' He paused, searching a mental dictionary. Did he need the same dictionary in his own language? I've noticed that his English gets worse when he becomes emotional. Don't worry, I wanted to say. I'm sorry I asked. I don't need to know.

'Pippa . . .' He looked old all of a sudden, and it was my turn to feel protective.

'It isn't important, honestly,' I interjected, to bring us back to the silence that was so easy.

I could have finished that sentence with more words, but they remained unsaid. I do not need any half-brothers to make sense of my life. It is enough to have found a father.

CHAPTER 63

I can feel my mind taking shape around a sense of purpose. For the first time forward-looking. Forgive me, Jenny. Wait for me on your cloud. I will be there some day, but in the meantime I need to stop drifting. I need to start planning what to do with the rest of my life.

I spend every free moment that I have in the tiny internet café that sits, incongruously, in a small side street off the town square. Like a teenager swotting too late, but eagerly, for an exam, I have surfed through a rainbow of different vocations, hunting out job vacancies and defining the skill sets they need. I jot down the bare bones of my life in preparation for the CV I will compose:

- Oxford graduate
- Bookshop manager (self-taught)
- English language teacher (self-taught)
- Waitress (self-taught)
- Sister (self-taught)
- Daughter (self-taught)

And this is where I hit the problem. I have one tiny qualification and masses of irrelevant experience. Every ad I see sounds perfect until I get to the part which says, 'The successful candidate will have a track record in . . .' No matter, I bite my lip and think of Nick. We live in the age of transferable skills, he says, so I draw up a menu of skills that I think I can wing:

- Adaptability (I am still here!)
- Ability to multi-task (I have been two different people at once!)
- Ability to work to deadlines (there is only so long a customer will wait for his beer!)
- Ability to use initiative (I found my father!)
- Creativity (ask Ignacio!)
- Patience (I am Jenny's sister!)
- Decisiveness (Argentina, Greece)
- Determination (I am still alive)
- Reliability (mmm . . .)

I try another tack. I draw up a list of questions:

- What do I enjoy/hate doing?
- What am I good/bad at?
- What do people appreciate/dislike about me?
- Where can I visualise/not visualise myself working? (office/school/home etc)
- How important is money/free time?
- What/who do I care about?
- What have I found challenging/dull in my life so far?
- How do I see myself in ten years' time?

The answers are not forthcoming. No matter, I bite my lip again and I work at it. When I get really fed up, I email Nick and send him a tick-box questionnaire about me.

What do you think I am most suited to?

- Primary school teacher
- Editor
- Novelist
- Conference organiser
- Fundraiser
- Branding consultant

Or rank the following as if they were my innermost desires:

- To influence people
- To change the world
- To work with animals
- To use my imagination
- To be rich and famous

He plays the game, and we tap back into something we had in Argentina. (One day I will tell him about the game I wanted to play with Henry and Sally after his departure.) Usually, now, when I arrive at the internet café, there is an email waiting for me. Sometimes it is disconcerting. Sometimes it is as if he is writing to Jenny. Sometimes it is as if I am teaching him about who I am, testing to see how he responds. Sometimes it is as if I am learning who I am. Maybe, if I am lucky, he will give me a logo!

Then I receive an email that slows something inside me. I do a mental double take as I realise who it is from. The pebble I threw in the sea.

My dear Pippa,

Your card was forwarded to my address in Thame, near Oxford. I moved here when Frank and I split up.

It was so good to hear from you after all this time. I have never stopped wondering how you are. I know we have had our differences in the past, sweetheart, but there is a lot of water under the bridge. I have changed, too.

You speak of your father and I don't know what to say. You are right, he was not a bad man and I wish things had turned out differently. I believe we could have been happy as a family, and I have never understood what actually made him leave.

But this is too much, my sweetheart, to write about. If you want us to meet up that would make me very happy, but I will wait until you are ready. I created enough pressure for you as a child. I know it can't have been easy living with an alcoholic for a mother and I won't put any pressure on you now. It is enough that I have my daughter back in my life.

Love, Mother

Her words are an uncanny echo of my own thoughts about my father. I do not recognise the mother of my childhood in these lines. Has she really left the alcohol behind? Has she really changed? What made her and Frank finally split up? Did the truth dawn through the drink in the end? Does she really not know why Father left?

I feel the same lame tide again, wanting to reach out and wash away the scars, but then another pebble slips into the sea. Does she really care that much? What about Jenny? If she really cares, how can she say nothing?

I struggle with ghosts in my heart and delay my reply. This deadline can wait.

CHAPTER 64

But another deadline is approaching. Andreas and Carla sat me down yesterday and told me tenderly that there would be no more work for me beyond mid-October. Carla asked me whether I would go home to England, or to Athens to be with my sweetheart. Bless her, where had she learnt the word sweetheart? In a reckless moment, I told them that it is my father that I go to see; my father, who is a Greek lawyer in Athens. Andreas smiled with a sort of misplaced pride, but his wife's eyes clouded. I felt a sudden urge, with my confession in the open, to bring my father here. As if I needed someone to witness us together, as if I was afraid of waking up one day to find I had imagined him. I don't ask to step into his world or change his life, but I wanted to bring him into mine, just once before I leave. I tried to explain to the homely couple before me that my father and I have been reunited after a long separation and that we are still getting to know each other. I told them it would mean a lot to me to invite him here and for him to meet the couple who have been so good to me. Carla looked worried, but Andreas leant forward, touching her elbow to reassure her. But of course he must come, he said. And so I have emailed my father and am awaiting his reply.

There are five emails for me the following day in the internet café. Two sender addresses I recognise: my father's and Nick's. The others will no doubt be just more job rejections. I could wallpaper any bedroom I could afford to rent with them. My father's is brief and empties my stomach. 'Yes, I will come.' I love the stark economy of the way he uses English, and I wish I knew Greek well enough to know whether he is the same in his own language. I am sure he is.

High and immune to the prospect of rejection, I flit next to the three unknown senders, leaving Nick's email till last, like the prize mouthful of food you save until you have finished all your vegetables. The first is a confirmation of my ticket purchase. The second and third are the predicted rejections. Oh well, something will show up . . . Nick's email is a test.

Dear Charles,

(Every email he has sent has teased me with a different name.)

This name suits you better than Pippa, which should be kept for dolls and pet parrots. Charles, on the other hand, stands for everything you could possibly want in a good mate and because I know you well enough to know that pride will stop you asking for help, and I'm guessing you have bugger-all to fall back on in your English bank account and probably haven't quite amassed a fortune under your Greek mattress, I am going to make you a proposition I won't let you refuse.

I have a spare room, no strings attached, which you can use as a base for as long as you want. You haven't seen my flat. It's not a bad little place. It's on the right side of the river (Highgate) and the Essex flats are close

*enough for a weekend away that will remind you (nearly) of Patagonia.
So how about it, Pips?*

*Oh, and in case you're wondering about Mel and how she will take it,
there's no need. She went off in search of a nineties man with no hang-
ups about commitment.*

I remain, truly yours,
Nick

What is it in me that resists his generosity? How does he know I will
try and resist it? Why not, after all? This is not like moving into
Ignacio's apartment. Nick and I are mates. Why shouldn't I call on
his friendship? What the hell am I going to do until I can get a job
and some money together anyway? OK, Nick, I will take you up on
your offer. I write just four words. 'Yes, I will come.' What will he
make of that? I smile as I click 'send'.

CHAPTER 65

The sun is low in an orange sky. Heather stretches, blurred, into distant hills, and below us now is the sea, a dark desert in the shadow of sunset. We have walked off our long lunch and the strain of well-meant small talk. My taverna owners were kind, and the whole family lunched together to celebrate my father's presence. The atmosphere was cheerful, my father was bright and grateful, and yet there was something slippery under the surface of our conversation.

A breeze seems to rise up from the sea and rushes to meet us as we move with quickening steps back to the town before the light fails. My father is to stay overnight in a hostel in the town centre and we have the whole evening ahead of us still. I battle with the rat at my feet, conscious that this may be our last meeting for a long time and yet, aware that this is a beginning not an end, I am torn between broaching the subject of Mother and letting it go.

Later, we are sitting in a taverna, picking lazily at olives and a menu of fragmented conversation. There are moments when the worried look returns to my father's face and I can feel a niggling tension at the back of my neck.

'Will you come and visit me in England?' I ask. I need to show that this is not a goodbye. There is no need for it to be a goodbye, is there?

'It is a long time since I went to England,' he answers – or doesn't.

This is not like him. This is too political.

'Have you been back since you left Mother?' A momentary flash of resentment is enough to release the words.

'No,' he pauses. 'No, I have not.' He is back to simplicity and directness again. Thank God for that.

'You probably wouldn't recognise it,' I say, becoming the politician myself now. 'Did you like living there?'

'At first it was difficult,' he laughs. 'You English are difficult at first! I didn't know what anyone thought about me. Then people started making jokes about me to my face and I learnt that that was your English compliment – the way you say to a person that you like them and accept them!'

'Yes, I suppose we are a bit anal like that.' I laugh to myself, thinking of Nick. Very anal – and yet that was exactly the kind of thing I missed when I lived in Argentina.

'A bit *anal*?'

'Forget it,' I say, laughing and filling our glasses.

'Ah, you see, you are English too!'

'Why?' I am mock-hurt.

'When anything gets too difficult, even if it is emotional or just explanations, you say forget it and you bury your shovel in the sand.'

'Head, not shovel!'

'No matter, it all goes in the sand.'

We are both laughing and the irony slips away unnoticed.

'Next time you will meet my family. I promise you that. It was just this time, too quick for me. Do you understand that?'

Your other family, I think, but yes, I do understand that. How could I not? It took me over a year to get to Iguazu Falls. It has taken me my lifetime so far to find him. But there will be a next time.

'Yes, I do understand,' I say, and suddenly that worried look is in his eyes again.

'You are very honest, aren't you?'

I think about that. Am I? I can be. I can also be very dishonest. 'I am, sometimes.' That, at least, is true.

'And do you hope people to be honest with you?'

Hope, expect, want? I wonder what the word is in his own language. Do I?

It didn't happen. We will never speak about it again. It didn't happen.

Yes, I suppose I do. Why, what is he getting at? I feel for a second like a mouse with a cat, until I remember that my father is a lion who does not kill his prey. Whatever my mother had us believe, this man's eyes cannot have changed that much with age. Can they? I nod but say nothing.

'Do you really want to know?'

'Know what?' I feel like a nine-year-old child all of a sudden, playing for time. I look sideways for Jenny out of a habit that will never die.

'Pippa.' He pauses and I imagine an old set of balancing scales behind his frown. 'I do not know what is the right thing to say or not to say in this situation. I never hoped to meet you.'

Hoped, expected, wanted? My mind is going blank, I can feel it disappearing, becoming just a desert where words blow past without leaving any prints in the sand. But I do want to know. I have always wanted to know. More than Jenny. This is one secret that Pippa always wanted someone to tell.

'Yes, Dad, I do want to know.' It is the first time I have called him Dad. In my mind he is always 'my father', but it slips out of me, responding to the moment.

He looks down then and up again with very still eyes. 'Pippa, I am not your father.'

What? *It didn't happen. We will never speak about it again. It didn't happen. I am not your father. It didn't happen. I am not your father. We will never speak about it again. See you Sunday. See you some day. It didn't happen.*

'Pippa, my dear thing, don't cry.'

So I try to laugh. I laugh for all the times that Mother has cursed this man, for all the parts we have imagined for ourselves in the Greek myths we devoured as children, for all the lies I told Ignacio in my therapy.

'Pippa, don't laugh. I will tell you what happened.'

Don't laugh, don't cry . . .

'Go on then,' I say, in a voice so distant it feels as if it comes from the sea. And so he tells me. He tells me that he did a law degree and went to London to improve his English. That he met my mother there and loved her with the force of youth. That they got married in a village in Crete where his parents lived and that theirs was a happy wedding, and my mother laughed a lot. He tells me that he gave up his country to live in England, and that he was ambitious and worked hard for his career and their lifestyle. Sometimes she no longer seemed happy and he fought harder for their happiness. They tried for children that didn't come. He tells me that he is a man who cannot live in darkness, and that he wanted to protect her from disappointment. He decided to have himself tested to make sure there was nothing wrong with him.

227

'I did not tell your mother about the test. I did not want to worry her, but when I discovered that I could not have children, I knew I would have to tell her. I delayed for days and then weeks. She seemed so easy to break, I was afraid to break her if I told her, and then one day I did not go to work and I told myself I am not a man to lie. I will tell her and we will move on. I came home determined to tell her that day, but when I opened my mouth, she rushed up to me and told me, "Darling, I am pregnant!" "Are you sure," I asked her. "That cannot be. Are you sure?"'

And it dawned on him that she might break him too. It dawned on him that she had slept with someone else. So he gave her the chance to tell him who the father really was. He gave her the chance to give them a chance by being honest. 'Is there nothing you need to say? Are you sure?'

He told me, 'I could forgive her for being with another man. I could not forgive her for not telling me. I could not stay with a woman who was dishonest with me.'

'And so you just got up and left?'

'Yes, I "just" got up and left. That "just" took years to get over. I loved your mother, I only asked for truth.'

What the fuck is 'truth', I think. 'But what about your children? You have children now, don't you?' I fumble for flaws in his story.

'They are not my children, Pippa. When I married again, ten years later, the woman I married was a widow with two sons.'

'And Mother – why did you never tell her why you left? Does she know that you aren't our father?'

'Ah, Pippa, that I do not know. I told her that I could not trust her and that I needed to leave.'

I look at the man who was my father, the lion circling, and I think in Jenny's language, oh well, he has his limits. We all have those and my mother broke them, simple as that, but it burns a hole in me to think this. What a waste. What appalling and unnecessary hurt my mother suffered for the sake of truth.

The third conditional is biting again.

If he had confronted her instead of walking away, maybe they could have got over the betrayal and stayed together, and if they had stayed together maybe Mother wouldn't have become an alcoholic . . . and wouldn't have met Frank . . . and . . . and maybe Jenny would still be alive . . .

Then this man, this man of principle who is not my father, touches my elbow and brings me back into the now.

'Pippa, I am sorry. I would like to be your father but I am not.'

So, who is my father?

'So, what now?' And I feel like laughing, almost. That sounds like such a crass line. 'Do we see each other again?'

'I would like to, if you want to,' he says. Simple. Black and white.

She lied. He left. Do I want to?

'Yes, I would like to.' Grey, grey, grey, but yes, I would.

CHAPTER 66

Tomorrow I leave. Today I brace myself for a last swim. There are cold, dark currents, which tell of winter on its way. I walk in knee-deep and then dive straight in. The water is so cold it feels hot for the first few seconds. I swim and my body gets used to the temperature. I have the sea to myself and I savour it, the space of it, the depth of it, the sureness of its touch against my skin. A rat nibbles, helpless, at the water's edge. Here, I am at peace. I wish there was a way to bottle this feeling to take away with me, like a perfume I can breathe in whenever I need it.

I let the early morning sunlight kiss me dry and I walk, past the houses, past dogs and chickens, up and up to the ridge that overlooks the bay. My heart pounds gently with the ascent and I feel an adrenaline rush of optimism, the power of exercise in open space. How many dreams are born at the top of a mountain?

Mountains were Jenny's peace, or the nearest she ever found. Just as I tried to hold onto the feeling of the sea, I try now to fix this modest view in my mind, its smell, its colours, its sound. I think of that other dramatic view, water falling as far as the eye can see, and I think – that one was for Jenny, this one is mine.

I have decided not to add the date of my father's visit to my address book. The day I found him still outweighs the day I lost him, because I haven't lost him, have I? You see, Jenny, it was still worth it. I have lost a concept, that's all, and I have answered a question we grew up with. I know now why he left us.

Yes, there is a new question now but this one has no history, nothing to feed on. Who, then, is our real father? We know nothing about who he could be. He has no story. Does Mother even know that her husband was not the father of her children? Does it matter? I think of the world we live in. How many children die every day of malnutrition or disease? How many refugees can we turn away in the West without feeling guilty? How many times will mankind wage war on itself? When will torture stop? Those are things that matter. My family tree is an irrelevant detail. I acknowledge Ana quietly, bringing up the child of her sister as if she were her own.

I take one long, last, lingering look over the bay and then head down the rocky path towards the action of packing and saying my goodbyes, towards the next unknown hand in the cards that life has dealt me.

CHAPTER 67

But there is a wild card waiting for me.

I have been back in the UK only two weeks when it happens. I have even emailed my mother, trying to be gentle, trying not to throw the truth that I have learnt at her, telling her only that I am grateful for her email, that I will contact her again and would like to see her when I am ready. I always need time to prepare myself, I think, still envious of Jenny: time to lose my virginity, time to make the trip to Iguazu Falls, time to find my father.

I have been staying with Nick. Football! I had forgotten how important it is in England, a currency which guarantees an endless, easy source of conversation, as useful between close friends as it is between perfect strangers. Nick is not immune, and I watch in amazement as he devours the scorelines in the endless Sunday sports pages. I tell him Jenny used to say football was just men's way of talking about their feelings.

'That's where you're wrong, though,' he says, 'ever since Princess Di died, feelings are all the rage. You can see men everywhere crying and talking about their feelings now.'

'Are you really good at your job or are you just blackmailing the boss?'

'There you are, you see. I, more than anyone, owe a personal debt to our late princess. People just pour out their feelings now. It makes my job so much easier.'

'Nick, do you know what?'

'What?'

'I'm so glad you're not my brother.'

'Christ, me too!'

'OK, you don't need to sound that relieved!'

'You know what's so great about having you around?'

'Go on,' I say, preparing myself.

'The fact that you're not a sister or a partner.'

'You mean no ties, you can just be yourself, unfettered,' I mock him.

'Yes, actually, I suppose I do.' For a moment he is serious, and then he laughs. 'So, do you want to know the result of the match?'

'No thanks. I'm off to do my emails.'

* * *

And there it is, another rule broken. Ignacio has written to me. I pause long and hard before I open the email, anger battling with curiosity and an involuntary tenderness. In the end it is the plea in the subject line – I know, I know, I know – that opens the drawer.

Dear Jenny,

I know I agreed not to write, but you always said rules are only rules when they are broken. Bear with me, please. This is important. Perhaps there is no way back for the two of us, I accept that, but I still care about you and want the best for you and that is the only reason I have broken the rule.

Before Iguazu, did you trust me? Please, stop and think about the answer to this question. If you did, then send me an email with just the answer yes and I will send you another email. If you didn't, then say no and I will not bother you again. Please just focus on that question and that question only for now. Can you do this for me?

With warmth,

Ignacio

The wheels of my mind move slowly. 'With warmth' – how formal. He cares . . . it filters through the strangeness. Twice I have punished him. I see the look of pain on his face as I try to push him away before he comes inside me on our first night together. I see the look of weary resignation when I tell him it is over at Iguazu. Both times my need to punish felt bigger than me, bigger than the situation. Both times Ignacio was the innocent victim. In a dusty corner of the drawer I have just allowed myself to open, I admire his ability to move beyond resentment. Will I ever be able to do that with my own mother? Will I ever forgive the world for taking Jenny away? Why is she still so silent in my head?

The loneliness burns and, in it, I focus on the question that Ignacio has set me. Did I trust you, Ignacio? I remember how I struggled to explain why it had to be over between us after Iguazu. I remember in the end that he looked so shattered by it all he just withdrew and said, 'Do what you feel you have to do.' At the time it felt impossible to do anything else, but he was there, he was there beside me, he bore witness to my journey. Did I trust him?

Yes. I click 'send'.

CHAPTER 68

Autumn is giving way to winter. Wouldn't it be wonderful if human beings had the same cycle as nature? I think of Mrs Forster and how she would have relished another spring in her life, the folds in her face filled with flesh again and the languor of lengthening days to live differently. And me? What would I do differently if I had my life to live again? My sister's laughter plays in my head but it is just an echo. Her voice – the body of it, the flesh of it – is no longer there.

In Argentina spring is giving way to summer. Ignacio has asked me to go back. He has done it cleverly, ambushed me, much as I did to him the first time I persuaded him to let me meet his children, but this is not an afternoon outing to a city park. He is asking me to cross the world again. He is asking me to travel back into the past again. He is asking me to take a leap of faith greater than the height of Iguazu Falls, to jump into clouds of cotton wool. He will not tell me why. He says I just need to trust him: trust him and book a ticket.

The failing light, as I wander aimlessly through the streets, makes me feel like an outsider, eavesdropping on other people's lives through half-drawn curtains, which frame the onset of TV suppers and

235

children's bedtime stories. I imagine myself as the orphan in a Dickens novel. I come across a scene that would sit quite comfortably in this novel: four people in long, tattered coats warming their hands around a makeshift fire under a bridge and passing around a half-empty bottle of whisky. 'Fancy a drink, love?' shouts one of them, raising the bottle in my direction. I smile and quicken my step.

The world is made of clubs, I think. There are the big ones: nation, religion, race, class, gender, sexual orientation, wealth (or poverty), politics, education. But there are other less obvious ones too, like disease or childlessness. And then there is the world of taste: what clothes you wear, what music you like, what food you eat, where you go on holiday. Every penny spent or saved defines us as part of this or that club. We are branded by our postcodes.

I shiver. What do I believe in? What are my truths? When I wrote those goals at the age of seventeen I wanted to do something worthwhile with my life. Now here I am, nearly thirty and I have not yet discovered what worthwhile means. I think of Ana, what she has done bringing up the child of her disappeared sister, and I think that is something real.

I remember one occasion in Buenos Aires, walking past a group of homeless people. A little girl with cold sores was begging, holding out her hand to fur-coated passers-by on this chic downtown avenue. I dipped into my pocket for some loose change. A few steps away was the cinema I was going to, and as I approached the box office I was suddenly consumed by the most enormous sense of sorrow. The coins I had handed over were futile, their only purpose to assuage my guilt. I wouldn't even notice they were gone, so I turned and dug deeper in my pockets, pulling out a note that would make a difference to me, a note that the little girl had probably never seen. I fought against the sense of virtue that now lined my empty pockets. What did a random act of charity solve? This was no answer either.

Jenny never worried about these things. In a bad mood she would have walked right past, not even noticing the little girl with the cold sores. In another mood she would have crouched down and talked to the little girl, handing out money without even questioning how much she was giving.

Maybe that is what I like in Nick: his transparency. He couldn't care less whether someone is black or gay. He either likes them or he doesn't. I remember the games I played in my head about our relationship, I have a fleeting memory of a failed erection and I am grateful for the resolution of friendship. There had been a moment, perhaps. Just after I got here, before Ignacio had opened the forbidden drawer again, Nick had broken a date to spray me with champagne and take me out for dinner.

'Here's to a new beginning for someone who deserves it!' The Nick toast. I was touched. 'You're welcome to stay for as long as you like, you know that.'

'As long as I can stand the sound of other women's orgasms, you mean,' I laughed.

The owner of the knickers I had found in the wash had lasted only one night in Nick's world. Jenny – the real Jenny, not the Jenny I was trying to be – would have eaten Nick alive. I thought, with a familiar flash of horror mixed with envy, of the symphony they would have created in the room next door.

Nick was looking at me, and I interrupted his gaze with another question. 'Nick, do you think you will ever settle down?'

'Settle down? I hate that expression. I sincerely hope I shall never settle down, but what do you mean anyway? In most people's life handbooks I have done just that. I have a mortgage, I have a "good job", I have a decent collection of CDs.'

'Aha,' I interrupted him. 'There you are, you've given yourself away! The next thing on the list was supposed to be a stable relationship, not a bachelor's toy!'

'And what, oh self-satisfied one, is this if not a stable relationship?'

'Fuck off, Nick, friends don't count. You know that!'

'I see. You're talking partner, you're talking pre-nuptial monogamy, the beginning of the end of independent discovery, the big bad ugly C word.'

'What C word? Ah,' I realised, laughing again, 'you mean commitment.'

'Sshh.' He put a finger on my mouth.

'Nick, promise me something. Promise me you will never be anything but a friend to me.'

'Ah, you see you women can't help yourselves. You're all the same underneath.'

'What do you mean?'

'You're asking me to make you a promise. Promises mean the C word. I don't do promises.' He was laughing, but his eyes were serious. Rules are dangerous, I remembered suddenly. When there are rules, they get broken.

'That suits me just fine,' I said, looking straight at him.

* * *

But I can feel the value of Nick's friendship now, I can measure it by just how much I want to talk to him about the dilemma that Ignacio has thrown at me. Patience; he will be back in two days and Ignacio has told me not to reply before seven days have passed. I feel as submissive as a cat.

CHAPTER 69

If it had been me pregnant with Johnny's child would I have had it? Yes, I think so. I would have had the child no matter who the father was. I don't think I could go through what Jenny went through.

I look away from the window of my reverie and pull myself back to the job vacancies in the paper in front of me. Whatever I decide to do about the Argentina challenge – and yes, there is a challenge in the gaps between Ignacio's words – my Greek money is not going to last forever, and the need to find work is pressing.

A shuffling, spluttering sound announces the arrival of Nick into his Sunday morning kitchen. I cooked a meal for him last night, which seemed to shock him slightly, but he ate well. I told him about Ignacio's email. I was clumsy about it, felt awkward and unable to really fathom why. I expected a tirade of some sort, a heavy dose of taking the piss before Nick settled into a meaningful conversation, but he was surprisingly thoughtful from the outset and wouldn't commit to an opinion.

'You said you trust him,' Nick said, pouring tea. His tone verged on accusatory, and I put the paper to one side.

'Yes,' I say slowly.

'Well, that's irrelevant, in my book.'

'What do you mean?' I say, again slowly.

'I've been thinking about it. It's the wrong question. Maybe it's a given that there needs to be this layer of trust,' – he almost spits the word – 'but that shouldn't be the reason to make you go.'

I wonder if Nick will ever trust himself enough to try and form a lasting relationship. 'So, what's the right question?' I ask, trying to keep the defensiveness out of my voice.

'Do you want to know why?'

'You mean why Ignacio has asked me to go?' I'm not sure that I'm following Nick.

'Exactly. It might all just be a ruse to get back into your knickers. It might just be a form of revenge, the only way he can move on –'

'No, I don't think that's it.' I interrupt, but Nick waves at me impatiently.

'The point is, whatever the answer is – maybe he's made some earth-shattering psychological discovery about the grieving process for a twin –' he waves away my expression again. 'The point is that the answer itself is not what you need to judge the value of right now. What you need to judge is the question. How badly do you want to know why?'

I am thoughtful, understanding him at last. 'You know, I have this image sometimes of a rat nibbling at my feet and the only place I can escape is in the water. I think that's why I've always loved swimming so much.' I pause, aware of how strange this must sound, but Nick is listening. 'God knows what that is about,' I try to laugh it away, 'my dark side or something . . .'

'So,' Nick says slowly, without laughing, 'why don't you go to Argentina?'

'I don't know. Of course I want to know what the hell this is all about, but I suppose I'm also afraid of what I'll feel. I mean about Ignacio.' My words flounder, but Nick doesn't rescue me and I force myself to fill the silence. 'It wasn't really me that Ignacio had a relationship with. He knows nothing about the real me.'

'So?'

I delve into unknown territory and imagine Jenny laughing at the fact that I am having this conversation with Nick, of all people. 'Well I suppose I'm scared of finding out that I still care. About him, I mean, about Ignacio.' I wanted the first orgasm to be perfect, but it happened while I was pushing him away against a backdrop of red velvet walls.

'Funny that.' Nick touches me momentarily on the cheek and I recognise the gesture from a night in Greece before I knew any of this was coming. Again there is the shadow of something that could have been. Perhaps I am imagining it, perhaps this is the territory of true friendship, but it is the gentlest of shadows.

'What's funny?' I say quietly.

'Well, I used to know this girl called Jenny. She was vivacious, unpredictable, mysterious, slightly off the wall. In some ways she was quite like you, but harder – harder and sadder.' He checks my face to see if he should go on. I nod. 'Well, there was this huge rat at her feet – not invisible at all! But she would never acknowledge its presence, always refused to introduce it. She carried it around with her, like a dog at heel. I think in a way she even grew quite fond of it, and Ignacio. . .' He pauses and I look hard at him. 'Ignacio, perhaps unknowingly, nurtured this rat. Perhaps he wants to do something about that now, but, as I said, that's irrelevant. The point is that this girl called Jenny eventually did what she had to do, what she knew all along she was going to do, and when she did –' another pause and he puts a finger over my mouth – 'when she did, the rat left her.'

'Nick, that's a lovely story,' I say, ruffling his hair, 'but –'

'Do you want to know why?' He breaks in again.

'Yes.' The word is so easy to say.

'Then go, go before your money runs out, and if you need more I'll help you.'

'Thank you.' This is a word that Jenny struggled with, but it slips easily from me to meet Nick's eyes, through the tears in my own.

CHAPTER 70

My stomach has a biological memory of the Sunday I went to meet my sister at Gatwick. It responds, now, in exactly the same way, as if there is only one way it knows how to deal with extreme emotion. My insides seem to shrink and I am left with a hollow space, which somehow still needs emptying. I want to retch, but I know there is nothing there. At least there is no vomiting this time, but the butterflies are rampant question marks. What is this journey about? How badly do I want to know why? The wings in my stomach collide in a vacuum.

When I arrive at Buenos Aires airport it is Ana who is waiting for me. This is not a surprise. Ignacio has arranged for her to meet me and take me back to her place for the first night. A part of me is impatient – to see him, to get answers – but another part is relieved and grateful to Ignacio for guessing that I will need time to adapt.

I see Ana first, and in the seconds before she sees me her face looks older than it is, the story of her own past printed deep in the lines around her mouth and between her eyes, but then she sees me and the smile takes over. An obvious reality dawns on me for the first time: she doesn't know my real name is Pippa. I was vague about leaving

Argentina and she was sensitive and respectful, understanding that part of my story was to do with the death of my sister, but not knowing that I had somehow tried to become her, to bring her back to me by living in her name. I will explain, I think, blinking stupidly, and then we are hugging and emotion is spilling out in choked half-sentences with no superficial meaning, which only accentuates the joy of seeing each other again. She marches us swiftly out of the airport, and within minutes we are driving through the familiar sprawl of concrete into the heart of Buenos Aires.

'So, the one you were never going to have a relationship with has persuaded you to come back!' she says, her eyes fixed ahead and her laughter playing in the words.

'It's not exactly like that,' I flounder.

'Well, you two do like to be the centre of speculation. What a lot of mystery! Ignacio wouldn't tell us anything. Even Daniel couldn't get him to speak, but it's not as if we were trying to get him to give away secrets about a patient, for God's sake. He just said that it was something vital, something that you would find out for yourself and that you needed to find out for yourself. Sounds to me like a psychotherapist's way of justifying a wedding proposal!'

'We're not getting back together again, you know.' I feel totally out of my depth all of a sudden, unable to fall back into the easy fictions that Jenny could draw on, uncertain how to respond to this woman who knows so little about me.

'Hey,' she fills the pause, looking at me sideways for a split second. 'Relax. You are to stay at our place tonight and then you will meet up with Ignacio tomorrow!'

Does she know more than she is letting on, I wonder? What is this all about? What do I want it to be about?

'Ana, I'm sorry I left in such a hurry. I just felt so powerless and empty after that trip to Iguazu, as if my sister's death was truly real for the very first time.' The words come out unbidden and I am surprised, but Ana's response surprises me more.

'Don't be sorry, these are things that have to happen. Six months after my sister disappeared, I woke up one morning and hated Silvina. It just happened. It made no sense. Poor Silvina, she had done nothing wrong, but there it was: I suddenly couldn't bear the sight of her little face. I hated myself for it and the more I hated myself, the more I hated the eyes that reminded me of her mother. The nightmares got worse, the nightmares about what had happened to my sister. I tried not to learn about it, I tried to hide. It should have been easy, everyone was trying to pretend that nothing had happened, people still pretend they know nothing about it, but people did know. People cowered behind locked doors and pretended not to know; pretended not to hear when a vehicle pulled up next door in the dead of night and a band of men beat the door down; pretended not to hear the screams which would subside suddenly, smothered into forgetfulness.'

There is a pause as she brakes suddenly, too close to the vehicle in front. Then she is talking again, her eyes fixed on the road ahead. 'That was when I first met Ignacio. He had just qualified and he got me!' Her laughter is hollow and I realise, through the shock of her words, just how much a mask it is.

'He helped me understand that it was not Silvina I hated, it was the universe and, when it all got overwhelming, Silvina was just too close to what had happened, Silvina was the living shadow of a life that I had to assume had been cruelly taken away. They used to cut the women with scissors, you know. At first I just focused on Silvina and protecting her from the loss of her mother. At first I thought we would find my sister. How can someone just disappear? There was no record anywhere of her death, and we believed she was alive somewhere. We believed we would find her. And then one day I woke up and knew we never would – and that was the day that I thought I hated Silvina.'

There is a long pause now and words swim inside me, wanting to go and meet her pain, but none are adequate.

'Oh Ana,' I start, but she interrupts.

'You see, the point is it takes time, and the journey of time has twists and turns that you cannot foresee. I never really hated Silvina, it was just a temporary state of mind, and she became a source of enormous comfort and joy in my life. You've already seen that. So don't be too hard on yourself and don't expect everything to mean what it seems to mean at first sight.'

'God, Ana,' I say, powerless, but she just reaches over, touches my hand quickly, and then smiles and turns off the main road towards Palermo.

'Lecture over. Now it's time to concentrate on eating!'

CHAPTER 71

In the drift of an afternoon that feels timeless and vaguely surreal, after a lazy lunch with cold beer on Ana and Daniel's roof terrace, the girls skipping in and out of our orbit and Ana shushing her husband each time he starts to push too hard with his questions, I do a quick time calculation and decide to call my 'ex-father'. We have been in irregular email contact since I left, but have not actually spoken to each other. I have his home number and, uncertainly, I prepare to call. He has never told me not to ring him there and yet I know it is a risk. I don't know how he will react. I decide that if anyone else answers I will hang up, but it is him and through his surprise I hear pleasure in his voice. He answers my questions and then I stumble through an attempt to explain where I am to the Greek man on the other end of the line. I don't tell him of the mystery. I tell him only that Argentina is not yet a closed chapter and the lion is happy enough with that. Thank you.

I send Nick a text and then lie back on the soft, white cushions of my guest room bed, determined to process what I am feeling, preparing to order the butterflies, languid now, into neat little rows.

But I do no conscious filing as sleep overtakes me, the unanchored sleep of jet lag after a night flight, that forgiving space where the body simply surrenders.

When I wake up I am confused, a submerged sense of panic rising out of some forgotten dream, wondering in that first split second of wakefulness where I am and what time it is, consciously taking in the superficial details of the room and the clock and yet still feeling vaguely dazed. There is a quiet knock at the door and Ana comes in with the bitter tea they call *maté* to ease me back into the world.

'You have slept for four hours,' she tells me. 'I think that is enough!'

'I admire you, Ana,' I say, rubbing my eyes and continuing before I wake up enough to stop speaking my mind. 'You've done something so amazing, bringing up Silvina as your daughter, dealing with the trauma you went through, you seem so . . .' I hesitate, already starting to feel too awake for this conversation, 'so normal!'

She laughs then. 'After everything I told you this morning – normal! You are a funny one, Jenny!'

'My name isn't Jenny, though. I lied to you, Jenny was my sister. Pippa is my real name.'

'What did I tell you this morning?' She is smiling very gently now, ever maternal. 'Don't expect everything to be what you think it is at first sight. There are lots of twists and turns on this journey called life and they normally spring out of nowhere.' She does not probe or blame or even try to understand, and I am grateful for the simplicity of her acceptance.

She is thoughtful suddenly. 'Does Ignacio know your real name?'

I blush. I feel red-hot, as if I have just been microwaved from the inside out. I have been so focused on the decision of whether to come or not that I have not even thought through the consequences. I am going to have to explain myself to Ignacio – of all people. I feel cornered. 'No,' is all I say, bleakly.

'I think you are going to have to trust him very deeply to go through with this, you know.'

I bristle slightly. 'What is "this"? Do you know what this is about, Ana?'

She pauses long enough to make me think she does, and then undoes the impression. 'No, honestly, I don't, but I know Ignacio and he would not ask you to come here lightly, and I know, from my experience of him professionally, that sometimes he can help you get to places you cannot get to on your own.'

I think of my own professional experience of him and it feels as superficial as a postcard. I cannot relate to anything real in it and then I think of his first orgasm and how I still wish I had been able to save it, to turn it into something real – and shared.

She breaks into my thoughts and says, gently again, 'He is here, you know.'

'What?' I am completely in the present now, and angry. He's changing the rules. He's not allowed to change the rules. Why did he make them if he was just going to change them all over again?

'Look,' Ana reads the anger, 'he's not going to stay, he said he just thought it might be a bit less loaded if you at least made contact, and. . . and he said he couldn't wait until tomorrow.'

I feel like crying and I don't know why, and I am also embarrassed by the raw response that Ana has just seen. 'I'm not ready.'

'Look,' she decides to take me literally, 'I will tell him to go and wait in the bar on the corner and you can go and join him for a drink and then come back to us – with or without him – for supper. OK? You can do this.'

No one has spoken to me like that since my big twin sister died. I pull myself together, on one level still in awe of Ana. 'OK, tell him twenty minutes.'

As Ana leaves I search my reflection in the mirror for guidance, but all I see is a face drenched in afternoon sleep that looks a little lost.

CHAPTER 72

There are echoes in my head as I step carefully into view of the pavement café. The meeting with my father who wasn't my father, the first time I met Ignacio unprofessionally, both times I had tried to be the one there first, coolly waiting, not wanting to be watched, not wanting to worry that I might forget how to walk. I have another surge of feeling cornered, as if I have been lured here. It is a disconcertingly familiar echo of the first time we met at the restaurant and yet, I remind myself, coach myself, this is me now, not Jenny. I can let her anger go.

When I see Ignacio his eyes drop momentarily, giving me space. Then he is standing and fidgeting, and I feel bizarrely comforted. I manage to greet him in a voice that does not falter and I feel the soft brush of him as we kiss each other on the cheek. With a jolt of familiarity I take in his smell, a particular brand of aftershave, mixed with something else that is always there. I wonder obscurely if I smell the same as I did when I was Jenny.

'Have a seat, Jenny. What would you like to drink?'

We have not even bothered with hellos and how are yous.

'I'll join you,' I say, pointing at the open bottle of Rincón Famoso.

'It's a bit difficult to know where to start,' he says slowly. 'It is nice to see you again, though.'

Well, we could start with why you brought me all the way here. Or you could stop playing games and tell me whether it's the doctor or the ex-lover who's sitting opposite me. But I say nothing, and a small, withered part of me doesn't care if this looks like a challenge.

'Have you given up smoking?' he asks, pouring me a glass of red wine.

'I've never really smoked, actually. I hate smoking.' I can feel the intensity of our momentary eye contact as the words jar with what he knows about me.

'Ignacio – or should I still call you Doctor?' I put the irony out there on the table between us, trying not to turn it into a genuine question. 'There is something I need to tell you before we go any further.' I dry up.

'Really?' He looks perplexed, awkward, and the observer in me realises that he must have thought he was the one holding all the cards.

'I lied to you about my name.'

There is the flicker of a smile on his face that I cannot fathom.

'It was Jenny who died. I am the other sister, Pippa.' And suddenly, viciously, I have an urge to light up a cigarette for the first time since I left Argentina. 'You're the psychotherapist, you tell me why.' And I cannot hold back the note of sourness, and then I feel my eyes welling up, and I want to run away and hide. 'It just felt like the right thing to do. Maybe I thought it would bring her closer to me, but the whole thing was all a farce, wasn't it?'

His hand reaches out towards me, and then changes course and picks up the wine bottle. He speaks away from me, looking at the wine he is pouring. 'I don't think the whole thing was a farce, no.'

I want to read his eyes, but he keeps them from me and I no longer have Jenny's brazenness to search them out.

He seems unsure of himself, his professional confidence missing. 'Do you remember a conversation we had once about compartmentalising different parts of our lives?' I nod. 'Well, you asked just now if you should call me Ignacio or Doctor –'

'I was only joking.' I try to soften the crust that is forming between us.

'No, but you are right in a way. There is an overlap here for me, because it is both the man and the professional who wanted you back. Don't worry, I'm not setting out an agenda here –'

'But you are. This is all your agenda. When are you going to tell me what this is all about?' In my own ears I sound like a street cat with no fight.

'I'm not.'

His words bring me up sharp and I laugh then. 'Is this revenge, Doctor Ignacio?'

'No, not revenge. No, definitely not.'

'He who protesteth most –'

'No, trust me, it's not.'

He doesn't look away when he says this. I want to disappear inside his eyes – I had forgotten the deep, deep green behind the brown – but then I feel Pippa's blush, and it is me who blinks and reaches for the wine again.

'OK, we have a conundrum here and we're going to have to decide how to deal with it.' He has moved into his professional voice, and with it I sense the pupils of his eyes distancing themselves, shrivelling into safety. 'Rules are an anathema to you, I know that already, but we do need to agree some boundaries. You have proved you trust me by being here and I am going to ask you – I know part of you will hate me for this – but I am going to ask you to take that trust one step further. We are going back to Iguazu, Jenny – sorry, I mean Pippa. Don't worry, we're not actually staying there, but do you remember what you said to me at the beginning of the journey we made there last time? No questions, I would find out in good time, you said. Well, that is what I'm going to do with you now. And no, this is not about revenge, this is about you, not me. Well, mostly, anyway.' He smiles with a question mark in his eyes, and reaches for my hands across the table. I feel the shock of physical contact with him. His grip is strong and professional, but all I feel is confusion.

'OK,' I say, a sense of resolution slowly masking the turmoil beneath. 'I have come this far. I might as well go a bit further on your terms.' I pause, and he drops my hands. 'Let's talk about something else for a bit, shall we?' I say, trying to smile.

We try. We skate around what Ignacio has done in the months since I last saw him and he is animated when he speaks of an international conference he was asked to speak at in Buenos Aires, but fails to give any real insight into his personal world outside work. We skim over the surface of the sea in Greece and I fail to tell him about the meeting with my father, until finally he breaks through into the murky water below.

'Do you want me to come back for supper at Ana's or shall we call it a day for today?'

Yes . . . No . . . Yes . . . I don't know. 'Let's meet again tomorrow.'

I want the white cushions of Ana's guest room. I want to be swallowed up in white cushions like cotton wool clouds.

CHAPTER 73

The last time we took this flight my mind was a dictionary of synonyms for emptiness, as Ignacio sat beside me, the quiet witness to a drama he knew nothing about. He sits beside me now, quiet again, and yet this time I am following him. This time my mind is like a junk shop, crammed with incoherent pieces of history that just happen to have landed in the same place. Is there anything of value, I wonder, lurking beneath the dust? Perhaps Ignacio will know how to find it. Maybe Jenny will come back. She is still silent; slowly, deliberately, endlessly turning herself into a memory, like the waters that run and run into the Devil's Throat of Iguazu Falls. I remember the vicious beauty of the Falls, and a part of me is sorry that we are not stopping there. We will see them from the air and then we will land, get in a car and drive somewhere.

It is only once we are on the road that Ignacio points to a place on a map. He has been difficult to read, knowing better than to make idle conversation with me, comfortable in our silence, sensitive to my confusion and yet earnest through it all. There must be a burden of responsibility there, I think.

'Hey, Ignacio, relax. I forgive you,' I say teasingly as our road begins its path into the jungle.

'Promise?' He smiles.

'I don't do promises.' I try to laugh. I sound like Nick – or Jenny.

'Do you want to know where we're going to spend tonight?'

I want to be Jenny again, I want to tease him and ask brazenly if we will be in the same bed, but I am too afraid to go there, shy of what his answer might be.

'Tell me,' I say simply.

He pulls over and opens a map across the steering wheel and I lean into where he is pointing and see a name in print: Eldorado. It means nothing to me apart from connotations of a mythical city and, quite literally in Spanish, the dorado fish. I look quizzically at Ignacio.

'So we're going . . . fishing?'

'You could say that.' Right now he is grateful, I think, for the gentleness of Pippa.

'Fishing for my past,' I say slowly. The strange dream where I met Jenny again on the wing of a plane floats vaguely somewhere and I feel tired, exhausted by not knowing what this is all about. 'But I don't understand what we're going to use for bait.'

'You will. Be patient.' He looks a little nervous and I admire him for having the courage to do this, for having the courage to care after our relationship fell away so suddenly.

'How did Ana get over everything she went through? She said you helped her.'

'Did she?' He looks surprised. 'Very few people know she was ever my patient. She must be fond of you. It is hard for the relatives of the disappeared, hard for them to get closure, when there is no body, no record of a death, no end of the story. And for the ones who are most optimistic, in a way it is hardest of all. It takes them longer to give up hope and move on, and there is a kind of insidious resentment against people generally for what was, after all, a kind of complicity. Nobody knew and everybody knew. I have seen it make some people bitter, but Ana worked at it. She was the one who really helped herself.'

I feel small.

'You are working at it too, you know. It is wonderful to see the change in you.' He pauses suddenly and a note of playfulness slips out of me.

'As a doctor or as a man?'

'I'm not sure.'

He starts the car again. The blurred compartments are a relief for both of us, I realise, enabling us to sidestep the questions we are not ready to ask, freeing us, bizarrely, to be in the present. The vegetation is thick and tropical on either side of the road that snakes its way through to the town with the name of a fish. Slowly, it gives way to fields of *yerba maté*, the bitter tea that has been grown here for more than a century, and then we come to the edge of a town perched on the brown waters of the Alto Parana river.

We check into a small, comfortable hotel with a courtyard and fishing tackle on the walls. There is a moment of awkwardness as we get out and Ignacio tells me that he has booked two rooms and asks if that is OK. I say yes, of course, and I feel my neck redden and hope that he doesn't notice, but once I am alone in my room I am relieved and grateful for the peace of my own space. I let cool water wash away the red heat and I lie on the bed and listen to the crickets, drifting. I try to block out an obvious reality, but it seeps in regardless. There has to be some connection between this town with the name of a fish and Jenny's plane crash. Why else would we be here?

I jolt upright mentally. What has Ignacio found out, for God's sake? Is he taking me to the crash site? For fuck's sake! What the hell is that going to achieve? I want to throw something at a wall. I have an image of myself throwing the glass of wine that crashed and spilt blood all over the cheese that Jenny, Johnny and I were having for supper that evening. Then I was exasperated with Jenny. Now I feel the same urge to lash out – and the person I want to make bleed is myself.

Ignacio sees the turmoil in my face when we meet for supper, and I do nothing to try and hide it.

'Is that what this is about? Are you taking me to the fucking crash site?' I accuse him.

He looks as if he is expecting this – brace, brace. The small furrow that has grown between his eyes since I first met him sits a little deeper in his face.

'Yes, we are going to the fucking crash site.' And the way he says it makes me feel like a spoilt child again. I breathe in and prepare to listen, but he says nothing more.

'Why?' is all I manage.

'Because it will help you get closure – real closure. Because it is the kind of experience that has been proved to make a difference to people who have suffered trauma and grief.'

'But why should it make a difference to see where she crashed? If retracing her steps to Iguazu didn't make any difference, why should this?'

'But going to Iguazu did make a difference. It helped you move beyond the fiction you were living.'

'So why bring it back now?' Oh this insidious need for answers. Ana has lived most of her life without an answer. Can I not do the same?

Ignacio reaches for my hand again and holds it as if it is the key to another world. 'You are right, it might not make any difference at all, but then again it might. Just trust me, Jenny – I mean, Pippa. Go with this just for one more day. Just come to the site with me tomorrow and then you can leave and never see me again – if that is what you want.'

What do you want? The question hovers between us. It follows, meekly, shy, as we leave the remnants of our meal behind us and part, going slowly to different rooms.

CHAPTER 74

We are walking through a *yerba maté* plantation about seven kilometres outside Eldorado: irregular rows of leafy bushes that look a bit like stunted olive trees in red soil. I watch my trainers print their passage in the sandy earth. Ignacio walks in front of me. I didn't want him behind me, watching me, but actually I am barely aware of him as I walk. I feel – almost – as if I have walked through a plantation like this before. It gives me a surreal feeling of Jenny by my side. The waters of Iguazu took her away from me, finally and irrevocably – or so I thought. Is it possible that she is reaching out to me now from the wing of her plane?

And then I see it. Shiny and irrefutable: the wing of a plane. Alone, seemingly, on the edge of the plantation, the brown waters of the Parana lapping gently close by. Is this your wing, Jenny? Is this the address you carry with you every night? The strange dream circles inside me.

I walk towards the wing, registering somewhere, peripherally, that Ignacio has sat down and is looking away. I walk into the space that he is offering me, follow the glint of silver with my eyes and, as I get closer to the banks of the river, I see something else, something protruding near the water's edge.

Then it happened. The breath I was holding left my body and I found myself gasping inexplicably for air. Something seemed to be pulling me downwards. I felt myself sinking, plunging, vaguely aware that the air was above me and yet unable to control my limbs, plummeting deeper under the surface. I tried to scream. I had passed the white line. I was being sucked down into the depths of the ocean, no air, down and down into the devil's throat.

Oh Jenny. The carcass of the plane is rusting where it landed on the waters of the Alto Parana, a piece of it wedged against the bank. The wing must have broken off and slid into the plantation. I drop to my knees. You were plunged into the water, Jenny. My fit in the swimming pool – it coincided with yours. You drowned, Jenny, you drowned. Perhaps there is another wing, buried with you beneath the waters. Perhaps you took that one with you.

I close my eyes and I see with sudden, eerie certainty the panic of bodies fighting with the water, clothing bloated with air, blood and bubbles and mud swirling through the confusion. I see the look on a mother's face as she loses her child's hand to eternity. I see the frozen fear on a man who is trapped in his seat as the water gushes in and takes him. I see a high-heeled shoe pierce someone's eye.

I open my eyes, alarmed. Jenny, this is too much. I don't want your memories. Please keep them, keep them with you on your wing. But there is a momentum now. I am in the memory and Jenny is pulling me backwards through time. There is fire on the wing, smoke pouring out of the engine and a massive rumbling shaking the plane. And yet inside it everyone is still. There are no screams. No movement. Not yet. It is a surreal moment, suspended in space and time, a moment frozen in the lives and deaths of every human being inside the plane. I see the scene enacted around me with a clarity so vicious, so penetrating, it is almost as if I was there.

Oh Jenny, what a shocking way to die. I am so sorry, my dear sweet sister, my other half, my life, but stop, please stop. Her hand is pulling me down deeper, showing me, pointing at the wreckage of bones and flesh and metal. Enough!

I open my eyes and am surprised to find Ignacio holding me. I am sobbing, and with each sob Jenny is pouring out of me, away from me, again and again and again.

CHAPTER 75

We walk back through the *yerba maté* field in silence. Every now and again Ignacio reaches out and takes my hand without saying anything. I feel the gentle warmth of him through cotton wool, concentrate on my feet in front of me, willing each step to take away the power of thought.

By the time we get back to the hotel, my calf muscles ache. I tell Ignacio I want to sleep, and he nods and then shuffles with me, awkward and protective, to the door of my room.

'I'm fine,' I tell him, and he nods again and says he'll be waiting for me later in the hotel bar, just come when I'm ready.

Sleep rescues me, at first; I drift, grateful, as if I am swimming again in Greek waters. But then it takes me deeper than the Greek waters – uncannily deeper into Jenny's memories, as if this were her last gift to me – into a kaleidoscope of images, images of the crash site, images inside the plane and the river, distorted and incoherent. I wake drenched in sweat.

I have grown up with a presence that can read my mind. All our lives we could reply to each other's unspoken sentences, but this is too much. It is unnerving me, as if Jenny's last moments have filtered beyond her death into my mind and taken hold with a force so powerful they have almost become my memories. Jenny, I have my own memories. I now know with certainty that my fit in the water echoed your death in the river, but I cannot make your crash my own. Take it away with you now, Jenny, please. Oh Ignacio, what have you done?

I shower to wash away the sweat, and steel myself to join Ignacio in the hotel bar. I look at the mirror – see again the lost face of someone I barely recognise – and will some of Jenny's strength into the image in the glass. Ana, I almost wonder aloud, is this just another of life's twists? Did you ever have your sister's memories? Sweet God, I hope not; I remember you said they used to cut the women with scissors.

Ignacio is in the bar, patiently waiting, and I catch him looking anxiously at me as I sit down opposite him. I feel a tiny impulse to lash out at him, and I desperately want to light a cigarette, but I do neither. I just look back at him, feeling vacant. He pours me a glass of wine and I sip it slowly.

'How are you feeling? Well, that's a stupid question.' He is talking quickly. 'Obviously you're shell-shocked and maybe you're angry with me, too, but talk, Pippa. It is really important to talk now. Say anything. It doesn't matter what, just talk a little.' It's the first time he has managed to call me Pippa without having to correct himself.

'I don't know what to think or feel, to be honest. I just can't believe how vividly I can see it all in my mind.'

'That is very normal, you know. The site where something traumatic has happened is often a powerful trigger. Somewhere, your brain responds and wakes up. Sometimes it all comes flooding back in one go, sometimes it is like a jigsaw puzzle, with pieces flashing suddenly in front of you. With time, you will start to piece it all together, but it will take time.'

Of course, I think. Time. I always need time. 'It doesn't feel normal,' I say blankly.

'Listen, I know this is hard, Pippa, it's a hell of a lot to process. It really will take time.' He is using his coaching voice, and part of me wants to shake him and ask the therapist to go away and let the man in him speak.

Beneath the surface there is a sheet of ice waiting to crack. I am not aware of it properly at first, yet there is something odd about the way Ignacio is talking to me; the way he has accepted so readily the infiltration – the invasion – of Jenny's last moments in my mind. He is trying so hard to make me think it is normal. Can it really be normal to remember your sister's death as if it is your own? I look at Ignacio over the ice sheet and he speaks again.

'Do you remember any of what happened afterwards?'

'You mean after my fit?' I say it almost dreamily. 'I told you before, no. I came to in the hospital. The doctors just told me I'd had a fit in the water. They did tests, but they couldn't work out what caused it. Of course, I knew as soon as Jenny didn't get off the plane, but,' I pause, forcing myself to voice the connection I now understand for the first time, 'I never knew until now that she drowned.'

Ignacio looks extremely nervous all of a sudden, and I want to reach out and take his hand for a change, and tell him it will all be OK. I try to soothe him with words instead.

'Look, it all makes more sense now, and maybe you're right and that will make it easier to live with. I am grateful to you, Ignacio, for bringing me here. I was always too scared to do too much research into the crash myself. I didn't think I could cope with the details of how she died. Well, now I know exactly. The plane crashed in the river and she drowned. The only bit I find really weird is the sense of déjà vu I felt when I saw the plane.'

I stop because Ignacio looks as if he's seen a ghost.

CHAPTER 76

There are moments in life when time freezes. A French lorry is driving late at night on the wrong side of a road in England. A couple are driving back from a pub, they round a corner and see the lorry. Time stops while the man decides what to do, trying to calculate whether to veer to the wrong side of the road, understanding that if he swerves and the lorry swerves too, they will hit each other regardless. The woman is still; she sees her life like the cliché, unrolling before her eyes, in the elasticity of imminent death. I am like the girl in the car in this time-frozen moment. I don't have control of the wheel; it is pointless to decide which way to veer. I look at the lorry coming towards me and nothing happens.

I blink and become conscious of Ignacio again. He is looking intently at me; he looks like the driver, as if he is trying to decide what to do.

'What's wrong?' I ask him.

'Jen– Pippa, you haven't understood.' He is speaking so quietly I lean in towards him over our drinks.

And then the ice sheet cracks.

'It was you, Pippa. You were on that plane. Pippa, you *survived* the crash. There were thirty people on board and nineteen of you survived. It was your name on the passenger list. They are *your* memories, Pippa.'

I feel the pieces of ice veering off in different directions inside me. The noise is deafening, and suddenly it is the noise of the plane and I close my eyes and I see it all happening again – the same expressions, the same horror gallery of images – and the impossible truth of what Ignacio has just said is thumping in my brain. Nothing makes sense now. Nothing will ever make sense again.

I am gasping for breath, and there is a single sharp piece of ice forcing itself into my consciousness. Words find their way, at last. 'But if that was me, where is Jenny?'

He is silent, wrestling with something I cannot see. I look at him for answers and finally he speaks. 'There is no Jenny, Pippa. There never was a Jenny. I believe you have something called dissociative identity disorder. It used to be called multiple personality disorder. It is characterised by different personality states, distinct identities, which recurrently take control of someone's behaviour. It can be a childhood response to abuse or some other trauma. It is often accompanied by bouts of amnesia, but memory can be triggered, and with memory comes acceptance, and you can get support to help you through this.'

I stare blankly at the textbook sitting opposite me and wonder what relationship all this could possibly have with me.

Suddenly I am ten years old again, sitting at the kitchen table with Jenny, and Jenny has just told Mother about Frank and Mother is screaming at me.

'Pippa! Is this true? Are you saying this is true?' I must have given some form of response.

'No!'

I watched more of my planet spilling onto the table. She fled from the room and Jenny and I clung to each other.

What do you mean? What do you mean, there is no Jenny? We grew up together. She has always been there. She was there when it happened with Frank. We were always there for each other.

'Is this true? Are you saying this is true?' I reach over to Ignacio. I want to shake him. He grabs my wrists mid-air and holds them between us. 'No!' The word escapes me in a muffled scream that echoes my mother's disbelief all those years ago when her mind rejected the truth we had given her about what Frank had done.

'Pippa, listen. It was a reaction. It happens sometimes, especially in response to sexual or emotional abuse during childhood. Your mind created Jenny. She is part of who you are, and then the trauma of the crash caused even more havoc and your mind responded with her imaginary death.'

'No. You cannot do this. You cannot be right.' The shattered ice is flooding my system now, as the tears overflow.

'It's OK, Pippa. It will all be OK. That's enough now.'

Behind the tears I see the denial on my mother's face and I am ten years old again.

What was she talking about? 'To be honest, I don't know whether you just imagined this or whether you made it up, but I do know one thing. It didn't happen. We will never speak about it again. It didn't happen.'

* * *

My father is not my father. It didn't happen. My sister is not my sister. It didn't happen. We will never speak about it again. It didn't happen. My world is made of water.

CHAPTER 77

Sleep dulls my mind at last, but I wake up with a jolt. Ignacio. I reach out, forgetting that he is not there, that we are sleeping in separate bedrooms. I reach instead for the bedside lamp and then clamber out of bed and into the bathroom. I feel nauseous, but I force myself to look in the mirror. My eyes are puffy with the effort of tears. I stare and I mouth aloud the narrative that has woken me up.

'You were abused as a child by your mother's lover. Years later, you aborted your baby. You left Johnny and you came to Argentina to get over it, and then you survived a plane crash. Jenny is your darkness, your comfort and your darkness. It was you who aborted the baby, Pippa. You killed the baby and walked out on its father.'

I look down, unable to meet my own eyes any longer in the mirror, hating what I see, unable to process the ramifications of this new reality. Be gentle with yourself, Ignacio said. He wants me to take some time out here in Buenos Aires and go to see a psychotherapist he recommends (a woman). He has spoken to Ana and she has offered me the room with the soft white cushions. I can stay there for as long as I want. He has already worked it all out. He is handing me a male solution on a plate.

Ana lost her sister and there was never a body. Jenny has no body either. I open the window to the stars and climb, weary, back into bed and switch off the light. I can see the glow of moonlight through the open window.

Yes she does, a voice in my head corrects. She does have a body. It is your body. You and Jenny are one. I close my eyes and feel the imaginary waters of Greece against my skin and I drift backwards in time, through the Greek seas and back into the childhood holiday seas of Mexico.

I love swimming. It empties me. There was a time we would swim further and further out, daring each other on, until the shore looked like the sky and white foam meant the end of the reef was only yards away. We knew not to go beyond the white line. We knew that the water beyond the reef would no longer protect us and sharks watched, but sheltered by the reef we were fearless.

One of us. I sink finally into sleep again, but I wake up at first light with a vicious sense of purpose. My brain has been working in my sleep. The photo Jenny gave me. I have it with me. Evidence. I delve into the bottom of my bag and take out the precious velvet pouch I carry everywhere. It is a long time since I have looked at the photo. I'm not sure why. I have a vague sense of it causing pain and of a lack of clarity over when it was taken. I take out the thin leather case inside the velvet pouch with slow, solemn triumph. In my mind I am already showing the image to Ignacio, already proving that he is wrong.

But what I see makes no sense. The photo is there and I am in it, and I look fresh and barely eighteen. My hair is windswept and half covers my face. My eyes look straight past the camera as if I am not aware of the picture being taken, but the photo is torn in half. I try and try but I cannot remember tearing it. Who tore it in half? Where is the other half? Jenny, where are you?

Time stretches and slows, stretches and slows, and in the elasticity of another endless moment, my body makes a decision.

I follow it, silently. It stops at Ignacio's door and knocks gently. When there is no response, it tries the handle and the door opens. The blinds are down, but not closed, and light filters through the criss-cross gaps. The effect adds to the surreal dreaminess of my movements. I walk over to the bed and sit on the edge and look at Ignacio, still asleep. I can see the little boy underneath the lines on his face. I want to lie down next to him and put my face against his and feel his cheek against mine and disappear in a grave of white cushions forever.

He shifts then and his eyes open and he sees me slowly. There is a moment of contortion on his face and I see that his own twin identities are battling: the professional who has diagnosed the woman he should not have gone near and the man who wants her, the man who is still recovering from his own failed marriage. I look deep into the dilated green of his eyes and I think that we live in a world that is nonsensical. We kill each other in the name of our gods. We destroy the environment that sustains us. We torture people for belonging to the wrong club. Relationships fall off the end of a cliff for no reason. Children are sexually abused and mothers deny it. Fathers are like fathers without being fathers. A man with bad eyes triggers a darkness inside the eight-year-old flesh of a little girl and the darkness becomes a woman who kills her unborn baby.

I remove my nightshirt slowly, still holding Ignacio's eyes, and as I climb into his embrace a rat scuttles out of view beneath the bed.

EPILOGUE

My dear Pippa,

Thank you for coming to see me. It meant a great deal to me. I hope you forgive me for not telling you about the cancer. I didn't want you to come out of guilt or duty. I wanted you to come because you wanted to, and that was why it meant so very much that you came of your own accord. I hope you understand.

I am not unhappy. My life has not been easy, but I have found a kind of peace, for which I am grateful. My days are numbered, though, and there is no point pretending otherwise, but there is something I need to say to you, my daughter, which I did not have the strength to tell you when we met. I do feel I owe this to you, though, and I have lied to myself so much over the years that I cannot bear to keep anything from you now.

There was something in that postcard you sent me, when you got in contact again. Something uncanny that has quietly haunted me. You said that you had found 'our father'. I couldn't bring myself to ask about that pronoun. I thought I was getting carried away and I was too happy to have you back in my life, but, well, here it is, my sweet – you were born with a twin sister. She had a hole in her heart and she died when you were four months old. I never had any pictures of her. Could it be that your subconscious retains some kind of memory of her, something that slipped out in the pronoun on your postcard without you realising it?

I'm sorry I never told you before, Pippa, and thank you again for making the trip all the way from Argentina to see me. It means the world to me, and I wish you real happiness. I must stop writing now, I am exhausted.

With love forever,

Mother

SPOILER ALERT

THE INSPIRATION BEHIND
TWIN TRUTHS

I love twists. Although we tend to associate these with fiction, real lives are full of them, surprisingly so if we stop to take stock. But in a novel they can create a sense of poetry that's often absent in the day to day of real life's continuum. As a reader and a writer I love the potential impact of the twist; the power to shock, to reveal, to make sense of chaos – or turn order upside down.

The inspiration for *Twin Truths* grew out of two things: the conviction that there is never only one reality, and a life-long fascination with the meaning of personal identity.

I was born in Africa and grew up in an aboriginal community in Australia, before moving to the UK and then Argentina, where I lived for nine years. I think this made me very aware of how different perspectives can shape people's subjective sense of reality, at both a cultural and individual level.

If you and I experience the same event, it will be completely different for both of us. There are many factors at play here: circumstantial, hormonal, genetic, cultural, or whatever else intervenes to define our personal perspective. But of course, it doesn't stop there. The reality of that experience grows and changes with time for each of us, a subtle metamorphosis we're rarely aware of, as the memory becomes a story and that particular story interacts with other stories . . .

And the biggest story of all may actually be the notion of identity. There is a lot of philosophical debate about what personal identity really is. We live in an era which embraces the idea that our individual identity resides somewhere within us, as if it is something almost static, waiting to be discovered. We are encouraged to be 'authentic', 'true to ourselves', and, once we have discovered 'who we really are', to use this as a barometer for the biggest decisions in our lives.

And yet, this 'I' we believe in is a tricky beast. It can mutate and have many different facets or phases in its lifetime. It can change according to whose company it's in, it can be transformed by drink or drugs or medicine, or be thrown totally off course by an unexpected twist in life's journey. Scientific research indicates that, given the 'right' circumstances, we are all capable of torture.

So this tricky little beast is perhaps easier to live with if we tame it and name it. This 'I' may well be the ultimate habit, comforting in the extreme, the story we unknowingly create to make it possible for us to negotiate the world and our relationships.

But what happens if something bad is thrown suddenly into the cage we have built for this tricky little beast? Trauma can break a habit or create a new one. And this is what led to the drama at the heart of *Twin Truths*. Sexual abuse in childhood is horribly more common than we'd like to think, and it can wreak havoc with a person's psyche. As I researched the impact of sexual abuse, I learnt that it could lead to a psychological syndrome called Dissociative Identity Disorder (previously known as Multiple Personality Disorder). I never intended the book to be anything more than a very loose and subtle exploration of the kind of things that could happen as a result: the way different identities can take over, as if one 'I' flees and takes refuge in another, the way bouts of amnesia can interact with reality, the ability to unknowingly create a different reality to massage one that is too painful to live with.

In a way, I see Dissociative Identity Disorder as an extension of something we are all susceptible to in one form or another, depending on what life throws at us. We take refuge, we block things out, we project an image to the world or ourselves, we create small worlds in our mind and then believe in them and make them bigger. Mild identity shifts are a facet of everyday existence, just as mild madness can be, without ever needing diagnosis.

During the nine years I lived in Buenos Aires, not long after the atrocities of Argentina's 'dirty war', I witnessed a kind of collective amnesia about the 30,000 'disappeared', a gentle collusion almost everywhere to forget and move on, an implicit denial of what had been seen and known during the dark years of dictatorship. Almost an expression – en masse – of Dissociative Identity Disorder, in the face of a reality too horrific to counter. The tragic story of Ana, whose sister was one of the disappeared, creates a poignant parallel for Jenny in *Twin Truths*.

Then there is the intrigue of twins. Both my brother and sister have twins, and my grandmother lost a twin brother she took years to tell the family about. Twins are perfect for an exploration of identity: the way nature versus nurture plays itself out in the case of two individuals who have shared the same womb, the strength of the bond and understanding between them, the way they grow up with labels that separate or unite them by turns. By creating Jenny/Pippa as twins I was able to explore not just their differences and similarities, but the power of the relationship between them and the impact of loss when one of them disappears.

Life's road is full of unexpected turns. Some are exciting, some are appalling. These can change us completely or ground us even more firmly in the essence of the 'I' that we believe in, but they always cause some kind of evolution in our being, always create consequences in our own personal story. In *Twin Truths*, what I wanted to achieve was an ending that was as much a twist for the protagonist as for the reader. A twist that exposes the elasticity of reality, creating a whole new version of someone's personal history and sense of self. Twin Truths – two truths; the truth the protagonist has lived and the retrospective truth that is discovered. In the end, which one is more 'real'?

ACKNOWLEDGEMENTS

To everyone who has been part of the journey of Twin Truths, my heart says thank you. My agent, Broo Doherty, for all she has done, for never giving up, and for becoming a friend. Lisa Hughes for her inspiring editorial input. Paul Swallow for the crucial part he played in the birth of *Twin Truths* at Cutting Edge Press; and Martin, Saffeya, Sean and the rest of the team there. David, Broo, Rebecca and Emily at The Dome Press for giving the book a second life and publishing this new edition. Jem for the lovely new cover; Aidan, Amanda, Elizabeth, Anne, Jackie, Nellie, Leah, Liz, Jo, Book Geek, BC, Mahima, A. Rhodes and indeed anyone else who has quoted or reviewed and given space to the book on their blogs. The friends and family who were brave enough to read and talk to me about the early drafts: Mum, Tammy, Deeks, Es, Sarah, Meena, Nic, Nicola, Andy, Nella, James, Celia and her daughter Sarah, Don, Tom, Delphine, Maria del Mar, Fiona, Aviva, the three Amandas in my life, Laura, Belinda, Sophie, Tania, Nichola, and Simon. Aidan Hartley, for his amazing encouragement and feedback, which inspired me to rewrite Part Three. Nella, also, for being my writing buddy and sharing some of the happiest writing memories I think I'll ever have. Andy and Nicola, also, for harbouring a tormented spirit at a time of need for both the person and the book. My brother for loving me enough not to feel he had to read a book that wasn't science fiction, and my sister for being, if not actually a twin, as close as one. The real twins in my life, Scott, Alex, Rosie and Reuben, who were born after my paper twins were first conceived, and their siblings Jamie, Ella and Indi. My mum for reading every version and supporting me as only a mother can. My dad for giving me the drive to suspend judgment and get it out – and for his blood, which lives on in me and without which I couldn't have done it. Bull for always being there and always believing.